Curse of the Frog Prince

Part 1

Written by Madam Crystal Butterfly

This story is for older teens and adults. Due to mature content. Including profanity and sexual situations.

The Frog

Table of Contents

I would like to dedicate this book to my family. For always being there in good times and bad. Along with being my number one supporters in my literary career.

Chapter 1

The Breakup

The early morning sun shined brightly over the kingdom of Enwayo as palm trees swayed from a strong morning breeze. Shadows from the trees danced over the edges of the nearby beach, granting it some desired shade from the hot morning sun. Famous for being the only beach on the continent that had pink sand, people from all over the world once filled the beaches of Enwayo. At least, that was the way things used to be. Now the beach was completely void of any human visitors. That was except for one young woman who was standing near the shoreline. The woman's hands were rough, and her dark chocolate skin housed several scars beneath her clothing. She had an oval face that was delicately framed by long black hair styled into several individual braids. She stood stone-faced, both of her large hazelnut eyes staring straight ahead.

It would seem almost a miracle to any observer that the strong morning breezes had not blown her into the sea. Her body, although muscular, was so thin that the light green dress that she was wearing hung on her like a sail on a boat. Her bare feet were covered with mud, sand, and debris from the forest floor. Looking down at them, she thought, *I don't want him to see my feet this way.* She walked to the edge of the shore and allowed the aquamarine seawater to wash over them, clearing away the detritus from her feet.

While cleaning her feet, she wondered why she was doing something so pointless. She would have to walk through the woods to get home. Still, she thought, *what he thinks of me matters, even my feet. Speaking of him, he should have been here ten minutes ago. I hope nothing bad happened to him.*

Her heart started to race, and she began pacing back and forth, splashing in the water. *What if he was… no, don't think that way. He has been on more dangerous missions than this and made it out alright. Once he arrives, say what you need to say. Then don't talk for too long after that and head home. Home! That word feels funny considering my home is now my hell.*

She noticed a blue shell underneath the water near her foot, stopped pacing, and knelt to pick it up. After standing up, she started to examine the shell. *How long has it been since I lost everything? Probably two months or at least I think it's been that long.*

She decided the seawater had cleaned her feet as well as could be expected. She walked over to a spot on the beach where the palm trees provided shade. As she stood there, she felt a familiar pair of warm arms wrap around her.

A male voice from behind said, "I'm sorry I'm late, Akinyi."

Akinyi did not pretend that being in the man's arms made her soul feel at ease. But as much as she wanted to remain in his embrace, she had to force herself to push his arms away. She backed away from him.

As she did so, she took a breath to calm her nerves before turning to face him saying, "Owusu, did you learn anything about my brother's whereabouts?"

Owusu replied, "Akinyi, what is wrong?"

"Nothing, just tell me what I asked."

"If nothing is wrong, then why did you walk away from me, and why won't you look at me?"

Akinyi told herself to remain calm as she slowly raised her head and looked Owusu in the eyes. "Please, Owusu, just answer my question."

Owusu was a young man with dark brown skin and a muscular build. The curly jet-black hair covering the top of his head was styled in a temple fade with a sponge twist. His large brown eyes had a glimmer of kindness. He was wearing a white dashiki that had black embroidery around the neckline and sleeves. An old, faded pair of black shorts covered the upper part of his muscular legs. His lower legs had several scars, the remains of old wounds. His feet were being protected by a pair of black leather sandals.

Owusu looked at Akinyi as if he wanted to ask more questions about her behavior. But it was clear something inside him told him to wait.

He answered, "Sadly, I have not received any message about whether or not the prince is safe. However, I have not been given any reason not to believe he is alright."

"Why?"

"If your brother had been killed or captured, the usurper would have made a huge spectacle of it. He would have used the information to solidify his rule as Enwayo's new king."

After hearing this, Akinyi allowed herself to relax. "You have a point. That tyrant would be dancing if my brother was dead. Anyway, I only have a little time left. Were you able to make contact with that old general? Ehm… what was his name?"

"Mobutu, yes, I told him that Enwayo's princess would fully pardon him if he helped your family retake the kingdom. He told me he would think about it if he does not get a better offer."

"Meaning the bastard is hoping the usurper wants to make a deal with him."

"True, that greedy old man just wants riches and women. He thinks that he is so wise however, we both know that the usurper will only offer him death if he does not swear loyalty."

"I guess it's at least good to know that Mobutu has not allied with the usurper. Anyway, I should get back before my jailers notice that I am gone."

"Please allow me to escort you back."

"No."

"Why? I have not seen you in over two months, and you are acting like you're not happy to be near me."

Akinyi's heart began to pound, but she reminded herself that she must be strong. *Say what you have to say and leave quickly.*

She took a breath before saying "Owusu, I am grateful for your help and all the information that you have shared with me. I realize the danger that I have placed you in, but we can no longer have a non-formal relationship."

"In other words, you want us to stop being lovers."

"It's not a matter of me wanting to stop being with you. I'm engaged, and I can't be like my mother and have a husband and a lover."

Owusu stared at Akinyi, his face filled with disbelief. Akinyi knew that his pride would not allow him to beg her or any woman for her affection no matter how much he loved her, so he replied, "I understand."

Akinyi, once again lowering her face so as not to look Owusu in the eyes, stated, "I'm glad you accept the situation."

"Akinyi, I never said I accept a damn thing about this. But sadly, we have bigger things outside of our relationship to worry about. When everything is finally over, let's sit down and talk about us."

"There is nothing to talk about. Our romance is over." She said goodbye, and as she started to walk past Owusu.

He grabbed her hand, causing her to drop the shell.

In response, she quickly pulled her hand away.

In a disappointed voice, Owusu said, "Things are not over between us. I'll be here when you wake up."

Akinyi refused to look at him as she whispered, "I already told you it's over." She turned away from him and began quickly running toward the forest. Akinyi slowed her pace when she reached the edge of the beach. The princess began to think as she spotted the pathway that led through the dense forest.

She was hurt that Owusu had not put up more of a fight to save their relationship. They had been lovers for almost five years. *Was I just a trophy to him? Sex with the Princess? No, he loved me.*

Chapter 2

Akinyi's Decision

Then there was Tuma, her bother, the only member of her immediate family that she had left. Her eyes filled with tears as she remembered the last time she had seen him. They had stood in the center of the massive palace library.

Tuma's right arm appeared to be seriously injured. When she questioned him about it, he put on a brave face, telling her "No worries. It just a scratch. The doctor insisted on bandaging it to prevent infection."

He had returned to the palace to rescue her, informing her that Enwayo troops were in full retreat. King Ofori and his army would reach the capital soon. He wanted the two of them to lead what remained of their armed forces to seek sanctuary in their cousin Bonsu's kingdom of Yeboasi.

She had refused to go with him, reminding Tuma King Ofori had proven to be a merciless killer in other kingdoms that he had defeated. If she stayed, she could use whatever influence that she had with King Ofori to protect the people of Enwayo.

He questioned her, "How do you think you alone can stop him? You will be completely at his mercy."

Akinyi smiled. "You forget, Brother, that that fool of a man wants me to be his wife. I would rather slit my own throat, but as Princess of Enwayo, I am willing to make the sacrifice if it will save our people."

He tried again to convince her to leave. When, yet again, she refused he told her that as they spoke, their troops were gathering as many of Enwayo's citizens as they could for the journey to Yeboasi.

With that said, Akinyi hugged her brother, feeling him flinch in pain.

When he got to the door, he turned and looked at his sister for a moment. He raised his right fist in the air as he shouted, "The enemy may be strong!"

In response, the princess raised her right fist in the air while shouting in reply, "We are stronger!"

Then in unison, they said, "Enwayo will prevail!"

After that, he walked out, closing the door behind him.

By the time she reached the edge of the forest, she was crying so hard that she could barely see the side of the mountain. Akinyi had never felt so alone in her life. She chastised herself. "I must be strong."

Considering how far away Tuma is, it should not surprise me that there is no news about him. Stop thinking! Just focus on getting back to your room before the guards notice that you're gone. The princess used her dress to wipe her face and blow her nose.

She followed the mountainside until she finally reached a cave opening. When she entered the cave, she found the torch she had used earlier sitting in a bucket of water. She then picked up the bucket and walked a little back into the forest. Akinyi poured out the water but decided to keep the torch and the bucket.

Returning to the cave, she lit a new torch that she had left for herself earlier and walked deeper into the dark cave while still holding the bucket containing the old torch in one hand and the lit torch in the other. The light of the torch danced against the stone walls of the dark cave while the princess carefully navigated through the rocky pathway. The cave was dark and gloomy. Occasionally, bats flew over her head.

The cave floor was damp, and her feet were covered in mud from the walkway. She thought *I wish I did not have to go this way to get back to my room, but it is the safest route.* After wandering the cave for what felt like an hour, Akinyi's path was blocked by several small boulders. Propped against the boulders was a large ladder that had two large barrels next to it. She placed the lit torch in a small opening in the boulders.

She then sat the bucket with the old torch on the ground next to the barrels. One barrel was full of water while the other had several unused torches. Hanging on the side of the barrel filled with water was a dipper. She reached for the dipper filled it with water and cleaned her feet. After she cleaned her feet, she washed her face, hoping to wash away the evidence of the tears she had shed earlier. She pulled the torch from the small hole where she had secured it earlier.

Holding the torch, she began climbing the ladder. After climbing several rungs, she dropped the torch into the barrel of water. Akinyi stood still while thinking, *Alright it's time.* As the torchlight was extinguished, she was plunged into total darkness. Akinyi closed her eyes. She said to herself, "Focus use your sense of touch." One rung at a time, she climbed the ladder.

Once she could feel that she had reached the top of the ladder, she lifted her right hand to touch the ceiling above her. Pushing against it, eventually, the princess heard a small pop. Using both hands, she pushed up against the ceiling. Almost immediately, a small portion of the ceiling above her opened up. As she opened her eyes, she felt a sharp tingling from the bright light. She climbed out of the cave.

Closing the cave entrance, she stood up and began dusting herself off. The princess entered a small rectangular space not large enough to be called a room. It had red brick walls and a dirty floor. There was a large rectangular window to Akinyi's right along with a staircase leading upward stood in front of her. When she finished dusting off, she quickly made her way up the stairs, and slowly

8

opened the door, which on the other side appeared to be an ordinary bookcase.

Hearing no sounds and seeing no one, she entered the library, which was a massive room. The bright morning sunlight showed through a glass skylight at the top of the ceiling. The center of the room was empty, surrounded by the imposing bookshelves that you would expect to see in such a large space.

Akinyi raced across the room's white marble floors until she reached the other side. In the center of the other wall was a massive painting depicting a bird flying through the sky with its head facing backward. Akinyi quickly pulled a small lever behind the painting, and next to the painting part of the wall opened like a small door revealing her bedroom.

She walked inside, closed the door, and stared around the large room. Sunlight from the double doors that led to her balcony reflected from the brown tile floor to the stone walls. The room had been her bedroom her whole life.

Looking down at her feet, she realized how much dirt remained on them. She walked over to the nightstand next to her bed. There she picked up a white porcelain bowl containing a matching pitcher filled with water. She debated with herself whether to take the pitcher of water into her bathing room and put her feet into her copper tub and clean up there. She decided that she would sit on the sofa instead.

She smiled for the first time in a long while as she sat the bowl on the floor next to her blue sofa. As she walked to retrieve a washcloth and towel from a dresser drawer, she remembered the guards and thought, *I better go ahead and clean my feet before they get here.* After using the towel to dry her feet and legs, she walked to the nightstand closest to the wall to retrieve a container of shea butter.

As she sat down on the green spread that covered the top of her large wooded sleigh bed, she began to rub the shea butter into her legs and feet, her eyes caught the reflection of a small silver letter opener shaped like a sword.

The sight of the letter opener took her mind back to the day King Ofori and his troops stormed the capital and took over the palace. The princess had made sure that she looked her most appealing. After taking what she hoped would be a relaxing bath, she sprayed her body from head to toe with her favorite perfume. She put on a long form-fitting blue dress, which allowed every curve of her body to show. Her braids were twisted into curls. Her nails and lips were painted a lovely shade of red.

The princess remembered admiring herself in the standing mirror in corner of her bedroom thinking *I look delicious.* She then grabbed her letter opener from the top of her desk and walked to the throne room.

She thought about how delicious she looked as she arrived in the throne room, gazing at her parents' thrones sitting side by side. While she wondered to herself how much time the former owners of those thrones had felt disdain at the presence of each other. After climbing the six wide steps that led to the small stage that elevated the thrones above the rest of the room. The princess sat on her father's throne where she waited for the arrival of King Ofori.

Akinyi sat there for what felt like hours, occasionally standing and pacing around the room, never moving too far from her father's throne. *Even now I am grateful I was wise enough to have my letter opener with me.* The princess felt a cold chill at the moment King Ofori, followed by a contingent of Generals and soldiers, burst into the throne room.

As they approached the throne, Akinyi stood so that the King could get the full view of what she was selling. She looked into his face.

His eyes scanned her from head to toe. Then they revisited her breast and hips. She recalled thinking to herself, *Phase one completed.*

Chapter 3

King Ofori

Akinyi reclaimed her seat, tucking her weapon beside her right hip.

When he reached the steps that led to the thrones, King Ofori looked at the princess with a lustful gaze as he told his men to bow before their new queen. Still sitting in her father's chair, Akinyi told the king that she had no intention of becoming his queen unless he agreed to her terms.

The king laughed loudly as if she had just told him the funniest joke he had ever heard.

She declared that he might laugh, but it will be impossible for him to marry her without giving her what she wanted.

The king laughed some more as he climbed the steps to where she sat. He grabbed her by the waist, lifting her from her seat.

Akinyi cringed as she remembered how disgusted she'd felt when the man who killed her father pulled her into his arms.

The king sounded very smug as he whispered, "Your army is gone."

He sniffed her hair before saying, "Pretty soon, I will find and decapitated your little brother. So, tell me, what power does a defenseless princess have to parlay with me?"

At that moment, the princess felt a strange sense of joy right before she quickly kneed the king in his crown jewels. When he was forced to let her go, she quickly got a few feet away from him. In anger, the king cursed her, as his men started to pull out their weapons to subdue her.

King Ofori, who was still in pain, waved his hand signaling to his men to stand down. He then asked in a calm, cold tone of voice what the hell she thought kneeing him would accomplish.

Akinyi remembered how confident she'd felt at that moment she smiled lifting her head and replied, "Your Majesty may have conquered Enwayo, but you have not conquered me, nor have you conquered hearts of the people of Enwayo. You may not take liberties with me without my permission." Then she held the letter opener to her throat as she said, "As I told you before unless you give me what I want, I will not agree to become your bride."

King Ofori replied, "You think this makes you look fierce. We both know that you're not going to hurt yourself, so put the blade down."

"What makes you so sure that I won't take my life if you don't agree to my terms?"

The king started to walk towards her.

The second he took two steps, Akinyi cut a small fragment of her neck. Seeing blood slide down her neck caused the king to stop in his tracks.

However, instead of looking surprised by Akinyi's actions, King Ofori appeared to be very happy. "My, my, clearly I was wise to pick you for my bride."

"Your Majesty, what did I just say?"

The king rolled his eyes in irritation before dismissing his men. As soon as all of the king's soldiers were gone, the king looked at the princess with an irritated gaze.

"Majesty, you are wasting my time and yours are you willing to make a deal or not?"

He sobered. "What are your demands?"

"I've heard how your soldiers have a reputation for— how shall I say— pillaging, raping, and viciously killing a fair amount of the citizens in the lands you conquered."

"My men have been fighting for months, and the winner gets the spoils. So, unless you can give me more than willingly becoming my wife, I see no reason to give you anything." Akinyi recalled how calm Ofori sounded as he told her, "You know you're very attractive. Since you're desperate to make a deal why not just use your body to get your way?"

She smirked, "And how long would that last?"

"Don't sell yourself short, Princess. With the assets that you possess, you could hold my interest for quite a while."

"I have heard that you want to marry me. I know it was not because you heard I am attractive."

"You think I want more than just your body?"

"I know you do. Enwayo will never truly be yours without me by your side."

"Silly woman, my army is the most powerful in the world. What makes you think it would be hard for me to maintain control over Enwayo?"

The blood from her wound slid down her chest as she said, "Your Majesty, do not assume I would waste your time with pointless assumptions. Even if your men are allowed to kill as many of my people as they want, Enwayo's citizens will never follow you."

"Princess, you would be surprised how influential a few beheadings in the public square can be."

"Don't kid yourself. For decades the people of Enwayo have only known war, and they will never bow down before an invading force unless a member of their royal family is married to the leader of that force. Because the people believe that as long as my family is close to the throne, they will be safe."

The King stared at her for a moment and replied, "You honestly believe that Enwayo citizens have that much faith in your family?"

"My actions are proof of why they do. So, in exchange for the safety of my people, I will not end my life, and will willingly agree to a merger with you."

"Merger? Such harsh language, and how do I know that you are not planning to stab me in my sleep?"

"I assure you, Your Majesty, that the thought had crossed my mind, being a sensible woman, I realize that I would not get far. So, you see, either give me what I want, or I end my life now."

He stared at her for a moment before saying. "I agree to your bargain, but until we wed, you will be confined to your bed-chamber, leaving only on our wedding day. Do you agree?"

"Do I have a choice?" She thought, *Phase two completed.*

Chapter 4

Imprisonment

She had put the letter opener down as he pulled a handkerchief from his pocket and handed it to her. The princess pressed it against her neck to stop the bleeding.

The king then extended his hand to her. When she took it, he pulled her up as he quickly grabbed her waist. He then pulled her face close to him and began kissing her deeply, placing his tongue in her mouth. Her right hand gripped her small sword, fighting the urge to avenge her father by plunging it into his neck over and over again. She pretended to be slightly, reluctantly pleased.

He smiled, and Ofori then did something that surprised her. He called his soldiers back into the room ordered two of the lower-ranked men to build a large fire in the large stone fireplace located in the center of the room.

The men gathered wood built a fire. Then, out of nowhere, several of my servants, escorted by the soldiers, arrived with my shoes. Ofori bent down on one knee and removed the shoes on my feet. He walked to the newly lit fire and threw them in, followed by him yelling for the rest of my shoes to be thrown into the fire. I was so shocked. He turned and looked at me and ordered that he will honor our terms. But I was to return to my chamber and remain there until our wedding day.

She felt her hand rubbing the shea butter into the heel of her left foot bringing her back to reality. Akinyi returned the container of shea butter to the nightstand drawer, stood up, and walked to the sofa, picking up the bowl of dirty water. She then moved to the double doors that led to her balcony. She walked outside and poured the water into a large pot containing a beautiful and very large pink hibiscus bush.

Her balcony was very large and in the shape of a half-circle with brown tile flooring. The railing, on the other hand, was made of gray concrete, and two huge concrete platers were sitting on opposite ends of the rail, full of pink hibiscus bushes. Sitting in the center of the balcony was a glass coffee table and across from the coffee table was a white couch made of bamboo the cushions were covered with bright green fabric.

After emptying the bowl, Akinyi paused, her balcony had the perfect view of the nearby gardens that were home to dozens of red and yellow flower beds. Each flower bed was divided by a white stone walkway, and at the end of the garden was a massive lake. In the distance on the other side of the lake, Akinyi had a perfect view of the mountain that contained the cave she used to sneak in and out of the palace. Despite this breathtaking scenery, the sight of King Ofori's soldiers milling about the garden area took all of the joy from the view. As she stood looking at the vista, she noticed the guards below her balcony staring up at her.

One of them said something, and they all started to laugh. Normally, she could care less what they thought but for some reason the sight of these invaders laughing at her caused a strange tension to build throughout her body.

It quickly got so bad that in frustration she threw the porcelain bowl to the ground. As the bowl shattered into little pieces, tears began to flow down her face. Not wanting the king's guards to notice she was crying, Akinyi rushed back into her room.

Once inside as she realized the source of her sadness came from a mixture of worry about her brother and, knowing she would never be with Owusu again. Unable to stay still, Akinyi opened her balcony doors and began jogging around her room. Then jogging around the balcony back to her room, then back to the balcony until she was exhausted. She missed her daily training. From the time she was a small girl, she had received the same military training that her brother received. During her imprisonment, she often comforted herself with the fact that in a one on one fight with King Ofori, she could kick his ass. However, this time she felt no ease.

She jogged to the desk in the right corner of the room. The top of the desk was empty, except for a container of ink and a quill. A cushion covered with the same blue fabric that covered her sofa lay on the seat of a straight-back wooden chair that stood in front of her desk.

Akinyi wasn't interested in writing. She got on her knees and opened a secret compartment in the floor under the desk. When she opened the compartment, it revealed a golden ball the size of a soccer ball. She wondered if it was pure gold due to its weight. Carefully, she removed the golden ball, rolling it from its hiding spot.

The ball was beautiful, and its smooth surface sparkled in the light. Her grandmother had given her the ball many years earlier. Akinyi did not know why nor did she understand the cryptic message her grandmother delivered to her when she gave her the ball. She had told her to keep the golden ball hidden and keep it a secret, for as long as she does, their family will rule over Enwayo.

Akinyi rolled the ball around for a while, staring at it. She enjoyed rubbing her hands across its smooth surface, wondering why the ball gave her family some mysterious power. Whatever it was, it did not seem to be working at the moment. She was being held prisoner in her room, soon to be forced into a marriage with a man who'd betrayed and murdered her father.

Akinyi had no idea whether her younger brother was alive or dead. The princess rolled the ball around for a few more minutes before rolling it back into its hiding place. She sealed the opening, stood up, and closed the balcony doors. Then, lying down on her sofa, she closed her eyes. Her heart began to feel much lighter. There was magic in that golden ball; she just wished that she knew what it was.

Akinyi opened her eyes and sat up as her door suddenly opened. She was relieved to see her friend, Delu. Delu was at present masquerading as her lady's maid, but in fact she was a Colonel in Enwayo' army.

Akinyi smiled and said, "Good morning, Delu."

Delu replied, "Good morning, princess."

Delu was a lovely woman in her early twenties. Slightly taller than Akinyi, her skin color always reminded Akinyi of chocolate icing. Her black hair, styled with a pixie twist framed her oval face, complemented her glittering hazelnut eyes. She wore her signature red lipstick. Her thin frame was covered with an ill-fitting yellow dress, too big in the waist. Carrying a small tray that held a green teapot and a single pink teacup, she walked toward a small wooden table surrounded by four chairs in the center of the room.

Akinyi walked to the table and sat down. Looking at the tea set, she commented, "I've never seen this particular tea set before. Is it new?"

"No, Princess, this is one of the tea sets that the servants use. There was trouble last night. A group of King Ofori's men destroyed a good portion of the kitchen and almost all of the equipment."

"Oh, no. Was anyone hurt? Were they drunk?"

"Only the cook was in the kitchen."

"Is Zumba alright?"

"Yes, thankfully. He was in the pantry collecting the ingredients for making bread when he heard the guards coming into the kitchen. When he heard all the noise and wanted to avoid trouble, Zumba decided to find a safe place in the pantry to hide."

"How did they not find him in the pantry?"

"According to him, for some reason, they completely ignored the pantry. Anyway, the strangest part of the story is that Zumba swore that they weren't drunk. He heard one of the guards complaining about having to destroy the kitchen of all the rooms in the palace."

Delu poured her a cup of tea as Akinyi thought, *this information is perplexing.* She decided to worry about the situation later. Taking a drink from the cup, Akinyi loudly proclaimed "Ugg!" She gazed into the cup. "What in Devil's name is this grey stuff you are giving me? It tastes like poison."

Delu replied, "That bad, Hun?"

"Yes."

"I was hoping you wouldn't notice. The doctor came up with it. It's an appetite stimulant. Everyone has gotten very concerned that you are not eating and that you have lost so much weight. We understand how hard it is to be confined to this room along with all the other stressors you are facing, but remember your subjects are counting on you. Not to mention practically the whole kingdom knows it is because of you the capital along with the rest of the country hasn't been destroyed. So, please, Princess drink what is in the cup."

Akinyi's eyes filled with tears. She had forgotten the thousands of people who needed her to remain healthy and strong. Yes, she had stayed behind and offered herself on a silver platter to King Ofori to save her subjects.

She then held up the cup and drank every drop of the awful concoction.

Frowning, she asked Delu, "That shit was horrible. Are you sure it isn't poison?"

"The doctor tested it on several people before you got it."

Delu continued, "Since you haven't brought it up, I am guessing that your meeting with Owusu did not go well."

"It went fine. But he has not received any news about my brother."

In a sad voice, Delu replied, "Meaning he hasn't heard whether or not my husband is okay either." Delu's comment hit the princess in the face like a brick. *How could I forget Delu's husband is one of the Generals who helped my brother escape?*

She said, "Delu, I'm sorry. I know you have been worried about him since he left."

"It's alright princess. Just like your brother, my husband begged me to leave with them, but my stubborn ass could not bring myself to leave."

"Don't be hard on yourself for that."

"I'm not, if anything, I am going to criticize the usurper. If we did not already know he likes to kill over half of the population of any kingdom he conquers, we would have left with the others."

"You're right about that, but despite me telling him he cannot hold Enwayo without me. I have a strange feeling there is another reason he wants me as his wife."

Smiling Delu asserted, "Princess the answer to that is obvious. The penis wants what the penis wants. So, don't trouble your mind with the semantics."

They both laughed. Akinyi said, "You're probably right, and speaking of details Owusu received news from that old traitor."

"Let me guess; he said he would think about joining you if he does not get a better offer."

"How did you know that?"

"The old fool thinks he is untouchable because when he betrayed your family. He was able to amass a small army of followers. But I would not worry about him. If he does not side with you, he is pretty much setting himself up to be killed. Also, have you seen those two jackasses who check to see if you are still in your room?"

"No, I haven't, but I don't think it is anything to worry about."

"I hope so, but if they do not show up at all, I'm going to have to look into it."

Akinyi replied, "Good idea. If you discover anything abnormal, have Owusu look into it as well."

"So, tell me, did you and Owusu enjoy yourselves on the beach? There must be a crater in the sand two months without sex. Wow! I know when I get my husband back, we'll break a few beds to make up for all this time apart."

"I ended things with Owusu. You forget that I am now engaged to the King."

Delu looked down at Akinyi with shock, disappointment filled her face. "Don't look at me that way."

"Your highness, what you are saying is a load of hot bullshit. Owusu is the one person in this world who would do anything for you. He loves you, and he has put himself in danger more than once to protect and help you. As for the King, what a joke! We both know that you would as soon slit his throat as to say good morning to him. Why would you do such a thing? And don't give me any more of that I'm engaged to the king business."

Akinyi looked Delu in the eyes, "I love Owusu, but don't forget the King killed my father in cold blood. If he finds out about my relationship with Owusu, what do you think will happen? I know Owusu will be killed. We both know it, so don't chastise me for trying to save the life of the man I love. Even if things go our way, and my brother and cousin gather our allies, and the King is defeated. After he assumes the throne, Tuma will choose a husband for me. Owusu will never be acceptable no matter how heroic he has been during this war."

21

"So, it was the inevitable that made you decide to end it."

"Yes, I figured since we have not seen each other in months, it would be the best time to free him."

"You let go of him but, did he let go of you?"

Chapter 5

The Insult

The door suddenly opened, and two men walked inside. Both men were tall with muscular builds and dark brown skin. They were both dressed in old green shirts and gray paints, equally disgusting and frightening. Their shoes were covered in old dry blood. One whose name was Agyapong had a face that was home to a nose that had been broken more than once. His long brown dreadlocks stretched almost to the center of his back were dirty and wild. He had the cruelest eyes that Akinyi believed she had ever seen. Almost every inch of his body was covered in old scars, and he smelled as if he had not bathed in months.

The other man did not have a speck of hair on his round head. His large brown eyes had a strange lifelessness to them that made him seem more monstrous than his companion. There was nothing more than a stub where his right ear should have been, and he had a very deep scar on his right cheek.

The man with dreads looked at Akinyi, and, using an aggravated voice, he asked, "Hello, bitch, you have not been acting up have you?"

Upset with his disrespectful behavior towards Akinyi, Delu shouted, "She is the princess of Enwayo, I suggest you show her some respect!"

The man frowned at Delu as he replied, "Tell me, how loud can you scream?"

Before anyone could blink, the man quickly grabbed Delu by the neck with one hand and lifted her up as he slowly choked her. The other man started to laugh as Delu struggled for air. Akinyi jumped up staring Delu's captor in the eyes, attempting to show no fear.

She shouted in the firmest voice that she could muster, "Let her go. I said put her down now!"

Both men laughed at Akinyi's orders. Delu looked as if she was about to expire.

The bald man said to Akinyi, "Sit down and shut the fuck up."

In response, Akinyi looked at her nightstand where her letter opener was sitting. Quickly, she rushed over to her nightstand, and as soon as she grabbed the letter opener, she shouted once more, "Let Delu go!"

The bald man still laughing said, "I thought I told you to sit down and shut up."

In response to having her demand ignored, the princess rushed over to the man choking her friend and stabbed him in the shoulder of his right arm, the arm that he was using to choke Delu. The moment the blade pierced his skin, Akinyi quickly used it to tear a large gash that stretched from his shoulder to his elbow.

Surprisingly, the damage to his arm did not faze him, with very little effort, he used his other arm to push the princess away. The sheer force from the push caused Akinyi to crash into one of the table chairs before hitting the ground very hard. As soon as the princess hit the floor the man who was laughing stopped and instantly looked panicked.

Quickly he said, "Agyapong, let the bitch go."

Agyapong replied, "Gyasi, you expect me to just allow this little girl to stand here and disrespect me?"

"I know she deserves to be taught a lesson. But the princess is the king's prize, and she is going to keep trying to save that maid."

"So?"

"So, if she gets damaged, his highness is going to be upset."

Agyapong thought for a second before letting Delu go. She fell to the ground, coughing, as Akinyi rushed over to see if she was alright. Gyasi said something about how they needed to do something for the king anyway.

As they were leaving the room, Gyasi stopped and looked at the two women and said "I hope the both of you learned your lesson?"

The princess responded, "Don't worry, I did. If either of you ever enters this room again, I will tell the king that Agyapong attacked me. Looking at the bald man, she continued, I'll also let him know how you stood there laughing instead of stopping him"

Both men looked at the princess, surprised by her response.

After a moment, Agyapong said, "The king is not going to give two shits what I did to that maid."

"Really? Then why don't I send for him right now so I can talk to him about it?"

There was a moment of silence before Gyasi replied, "Fine, we will only pretend to check on you from now on. Don't think we are doing this because of what you said. Right now, the king has assigned us an important task, and having to check on you has been getting in the way."

The men left while Akinyi helped Delu sit down at the table. Delu coughed uncontrollably. Akinyi ran to the nightstand, grabbed the pitcher, and came back to the table and filled the pink cup with water. Holding the cup, she helped Delu to drink. Delu took a few sips, coughing with each swallow. When Delu finally caught her breath and, stopped coughing. Akinyi scanned Delu's neck for signs of bruises.

Delu proclaimed, "I knew they were stupid, but shit if I knew they were that dumb I would have gotten one of those shit heads to choke my ass a long time ago."

"Don't say things like that. It's not funny."

"I'm not joking. Thanks to their fuck up, we won't have to worry about them checking on you anymore. So, it will be easier for me and your other spies to sneak intel to you."

"Hold still. I can't see the damage to your neck. Is it just me or did you notice that their behavior was weird? First, they were late. Also, normally, when they do their check, they don't say anything to me. But today they went out of their way to insult me." She finished checking Delu's neck.

After telling her there was no damage, Delu massaged her neck a little bit before replying, "That is strange. Also, I forgot to tell you earlier, Zumba admitted to me privately that he heard one of the soldier's question why the King ordered them to destroy the kitchen."

"Something is going on but what?"

"Not sure but I'm going to get started on finding out."

"Be careful, Delu. I mean it. Don't take any chances. Something is up and until we find out what it is, tread lightly. Everyone thinks you are my maid, and we have to keep it that way."

"Think I am your maid? Look at this outfit I'm wearing not to mention that I'm always cleaning up after you."

At that moment they heard the drums, signaling the beginning of a hunt that would include the king as a participant.

Delu stated, "Yet another odd occurrence. The King just returned from a hunt. I will be careful, but I'm going to find out what's going on. Also, I'll let Owusu know about all these strange new events."

Someone knocked, and Akinyi answered, "Come in."

The door opened, and a female servant wearing the same dress as Delu walked in. She was carrying a large tray containing Akinyi's breakfast; she sat the tray on the table as Delu excused herself. The servant placed the princess' breakfast on her table, bowed and asked Akinyi if she wanted anything else.

After Akinyi told her no, she left, and the princess uncovered the three plates before her. One plate was filled with a giant steak, the second plate contained bacon, eggs, and sausage, and the third plate rice. She picked up the empty plate and a serving spoon. *The cook must be worried about my weight if he made this much food.* She smiled. *The doctor's weird tea has not given me any desire to eat. Oh, well for all who depend on me, I will force myself to eat.*

Later that day, the princess had a bath drawn to try to relax. However, the tub's warm water brought her no comfort. She looked over at her table that still had plates filled with the food made for her breakfast. Akinyi had eaten as much as she could, but it did not change the fact that she barely consumed any of it.

At the same time, she wondered why she drank that awful concoction sent by the doctor it clearly had not worked. She climbed out of the tub and stepped on a towel. After she dried off, she decided that she would sit on the balcony for a while, trying to come up with reasons for King Ofori ordering his men to destroy the kitchen along with the strange behavior of the guards including their willingness to attack Delu and insult her.

Lost in thought, she dropped her towel, and as she was about to turn to reach for her robe, she was startled when someone from behind placed a robe around her. The princess's heart raced as she turned around and saw King Ofori, Akinyi grabbed the robe from his hand, quickly putting it on and securing the belt in a tight knot.

The king was a very tall muscular man with his dark brown hair styled in twisted curls with blow-out fade. His brown skin was home to several scars with one of those scars having permanently sealed his right eye. The king's brown left eye seemed cold and lost while the nose that separated it from his right eye appeared to have been broken several times, like Agyapong's.

27

Akinyi wanted to scream at him for coming into her room when she was not dressed. Was she that deep in thought that she did not hear him enter her room? However, she was smart enough to know that screaming at him for being rude might lead to consequences for her people.

In a very calm tone, she said, "What are you doing here?"

In a slightly flamboyant yet cold voice, King Ofori said, "You are mine, and I have every right to check up on my things."

She wanted to yell at him for referring to her as an object. However, she immediately remembered how unwise it would be to antagonize him.

Akinyi told herself to remain calm before saying, "I'm surprised to see you here when I thought you left for hunting two hours ago."

"A few of my generals were the ones who went hunting. I wanted to go with them, but with our wedding being a month away, I thought it would be wise to stay home to make sure nothing goes wrong."

"I did not realize that our wedding was so important to you."

King Ofori wrapped his arms around Akinyi, making her skin crawl. Her stomach churned. She desperately wanted to push him away. Sadly, she knew doing that would upset him, so she forced herself to allow the king to pull her closer.

As King Ofori held her, he replied in a calm voice, "The only reason I care is that even though I believe you will be a perfect wife, our wedding must impress my allies."

"Why do you think I will be perfect for you?"

King Ofori let his left-hand slide down her back, then started to squeeze her bottom. At that moment, the princess felt as if she was going to vomit.

28

She forced herself to try to hold back her sick feelings while the king said, "Don't be silly. Unlike my second wife, you're not damaged. She was sterile and, unlike my first wife, I know you're not dumb enough to produce a girl and expect me to be pleased and ask for a second chance."

"As they say, the third time is the charm."

The door opened, and another man walked into the room. He was a tall muscular fellow with rough dark brown skin and cold hazelnut eyes. His body was completely void of any hair. He was wearing a white linen shirt along with black pants and boots.

The King shouted, "Don't you know how to knock before entering a lady's chamber?"

The man's face dropped, staring at the floor as he apologized. "I beg your pardon, your highness. King Ofori, please forgive my rudeness."

The king released Akinyi from his grasp, but that did not remove the sick feeling in the pit of her stomach.

King Ofori looked at the man as he asked, "What do you want, General Opoku?"

The general raised his head as he announced, "My king, we need you in the council room immediately."

King Ofori pressed his lips together appearing to be taken aback by what the man said. This made Akinyi wonder if something serious had happened.

In a very serious voice, the king asked "Did they find it?"

"The former queen's room was searched, and nothing was found."

"Idiots, don't they understand that we are running out of time?"

"To be honest, my king, we may need to make an example out of one of them."

"We can't do that. I'm heading to the council room now."

After both men left, the room the princess ran out onto the balcony. Once outside, she rushed over to the railing. The moment she got to the railing; vomit shot out of her mouth like a projectile. The guards below dogged the vomit. However, as soon as they realized what had almost hit them, they started shouting obscenities at the princess. Akinyi ignored the king's men while she wondered what exactly the king was looking for.

Akinyi walked to the bamboo sofa on the balcony and laid down, closed her eyes, and reflected on what she heard earlier. *What did he mean when he said that time was running out? Does this have anything to do with what happened in the kitchen? Why would it be in my mother's room? I hope they did not destroy her room.*

Akinyi heard her bedroom door opened. A cold chill ran down her spine, fearing that the King had returned. She sighed in relief to see Delu followed by the maid who had brought her breakfast earlier. The maid was followed by the contingent of maids that cleaned her room daily. Serwa, the cook's daughter, was among them. Serwa was carrying a tray containing a golden goblet and a basket with something covered in a dishtowel. From previous experience, Akinyi believed it to be bread or muffins.

She waved from the balcony to Delu and said, "I'm out here."

Delu took the tray containing the basket and golden goblet and walked toward the balcony. Serwa left the room as one of the other maids cleared the table of the food left from Akinyi's breakfast. She stopped at the balcony door and watched as the maid left the room. When she arrived on the balcony, she placed the tray on the glass table in front of the sofa where Akinyi's was now in a seated position.

Delu asked, "How is your stomach feeling?"

The princess' mouth fell open, "How did you know that I threw up?"

"One of the guards came cursing into the kitchen complaining about almost being covered in your royal vomit."

Delu laughed, "I wish that your aim had been better. He declared that you missed him by inches."

Akinyi joined Delu in laughter, "Next time I will try harder."

"When the cook heard that you had a stomach upset, he cursed the doctor under his breath, and insisted that I bring you some warm milk and toast to settle your stomach."

Akinyi could visualize her dear friend waving his somewhat rotund arms as he cursed the doctor. "I agree that whatever that was in the teacup didn't work. But honestly…" She lowered her voice so that the other maids could not hear what she was saying as they cleaned her room.

"It was King Ofori who caused me to throw up."

Akinyi related to Delu the details of the King's surprise visit. "What do you suppose he is looking for?"

Delu looked seriously at the princess. "I have news for you on that front, but while I share it with you, drink the milk and eat some of the bread. I am concerned that you threw up the food that you ate."

Akinyi ate and drank obediently.

Delu took a deep breath, "You know that I have contacts all over, one of whom happens to be shall we say a lady of the evening. She works for Mama Cleo. Well, one of her best customers is General Di. During a recent visit, the General had been complaining that the king has been pressuring him to find a gold ball."

Akinyi's heart raced. She told herself to remain calm. She looked perplexed at Delu. "A gold ball?"

"Yep, and apparently, King Ofori is looking for a gold ball."

"Are you sure that this information is reliable? I mean what gold ball and what is he going to do with it?"

"I was hoping that you had some idea. She also said that he needs to find it before the wedding."

Akinyi questioned, "So he destroyed the kitchen and my mother's room looking for this ball? Delu, please if you get the chance check her room to see if it was damaged by those animals. Also, ask the cook and some of the older people about this gold ball. Have you asked Owusu …?"

As soon as his name came out of her mouth, Akinyi regretted it. Luckily, she heard the maids leaving. Quickly, she rose and said, "It's getting to warm out here; let's go back inside."

Delu picked up the tray and followed. The two women returned to Akinyi's bedroom. Akinyi sat on the sofa, patting the cushion next to her, signaling for Delu to sit next to her.

Delu sat the tray on the table next to the sofa, sat next to Akinyi, and said in a soft voice, "I haven't seen him, but I don't think that Owusu has any answers. The thing that troubles me the most is that they have been secretively searching the place since they have been here and I had no idea. My best guess is that now that the wedding date is getting closer, the pressure is on and they are becoming careless and making mistakes. Could it be possible that King Ofori invaded our country so that he could obtain the golden ball? Even the murder of your father made no sense. He was willing to make peace with Ofori, but Ofori murdered our King instead. And I am willing to bet that it was not by chance that the General happened to drop by your room while the king was here. The King is not as stupid as he looks. They were looking for a reaction from you."

Akinyi desperately wished she could just tell Delu she knew where the ball was. But she remembered her promise to her grandmother to never reveal the ball to anyone under any circumstances. Delu announced that she was going to check on the Queen's room and see if she could gather more information about this mysterious ball.

33

She lowered her voice again, "When I see Owusu, is there anything you want me to tell him?"

Akinyi held her head down. Almost in a whisper, she said, "Please make sure that he is ok."

Delu reached over and squeezed Akinyi's hand.

Akinyi said, "Tell the cook that I thank him, and that I feel much better. "

With that, Delu picked up the tray from the table, pleased that the princess had eaten every bite. Then she left the room.

Chapter 7

The Golden Ball

Once Akinyi was sure Delu was gone, she immediately opened the secret compartment housing the ball. She sat on the floor, staring down at the gold ball for a moment before rolling it around on the floor. As she rolled the ball in the light, she tried to see if there was something special about it that she had not noticed.

Akinyi studied the ball for about ten minutes before deciding to put it away. As she was rolling the ball back into its hiding place, it began to glow. Akinyi was shocked to see symbols appearing on the ball's smooth surface. They looked as if they had been carved into its surface all along, yet, Akinyi had never seen them. She had spent hours over the years rubbing this ball, rolling it around, but she had never felt anything.

What could this mean? What do these strange symbols mean? Do they have a meaning or are they just decorative markings? Using both of her hands, she reached for the ball to examine it closer. As she touched it, a sharp pain shot through her hands, and the ball began to roll toward her balcony doors.

The pain was so severe that she clasped her hands together, using one hand to rub the other. She watched in horror as the ball rolled through the double doors out onto the balcony. The princess cursed herself for not closing the doors earlier.

She closed her secret compartment and began chasing the ball. To her amazement, the ball's shape changed as it rolled through the slits of the balcony. She reached the railing of the balcony as the ball hit the ground with a loud thud and continued to roll toward the lake.

Oh shit! She thought the guards were sure to see. And now that bastard usurper will get his hands on the ball. As she looked around, she noticed that there were no soldiers in the garden and the guards that were usually posted outside her balcony were also absent. The ball continued to roll until it finally landed in the lake. She watched helplessly as it rolled into a corner of the lake covered with water but visible from the balcony. *Shit, shit, shit, shit, one of the usurper's people might see it. Or it might sink deeper into the lake. Fuck!*

She then realized that despite her fears, there was no guard in sight. Immediately she raced to her bedroom door, peeked out to see if anyone was in the hallway. When the princess was sure no one was there, she walked into the hallway and closed the door behind her. She ran as quietly as she could down the hallway, hoping that her bare feet would not make too much noise as they landed in rapid session one after the other on the cold gray stone that covered the floor of the hallway.

When she reached the staircase, she slowed listened for the sound of footsteps or voices. Grateful to hear only silence, she ran down the staircase again reminding herself to move as quietly as possible. After reaching the bottom of the staircase, the princess yet again found no guards in the hallway. She rushed down the hallway and entered a nearby room that had doors that led to the outside. As she entered the room, she felt a jolt of pain rush through her heart as this room had once been her mother's reading room.

Interestingly, the room did not appear to have been searched. *Maybe the usurper and his men did not realize that this was the room where my mother spent most of her time.* Today the room was dark, with curtains drawn. She remembered how bright it was when her mother was alive. The walls were almost filled with windows. Akinyi thought of how her mother loved that the doors opened to the garden; the only place where she ever seemed to be at peace with herself.

The princess chastised herself. *Now is no time for me to get lost in trying to understand my mother. I have to get that ball back.* With that, she opened one of the doors and slipped out into the warm sunshine and raced to the lake.

As she reached the lake's edge, she saw the ball floating in the water. *There is something strange about this golden ball. It changed shape going through the railing of the balcony, and now this heavy solid gold ball that I could never lift is floating like a feather in the lake. Thank goodness that it is floating. I can swim out to recover it quickly. Then head back to my room before anyone realizes I'm gone.*

Akinyi jumped into the lake, reaching out to grab the ball. As she did, the ball began to sink. She dove, chasing it deeper and deeper into the cold, murky lake water. As the ball sank, the water became colder and colder, murkier and murkier, making it difficult for her to see. Soon, she resurfaced gasping for air. She scanned the surface of the water hoping that the ball was once again floating.

Not seeing the ball, she took a deep breath and dove deeper and deeper. Her body was shaking from the cold, and her lungs began to ache. She knew that she should resurface for air, but determination drove her deeper into the dark lake water. Suddenly, Akinyi felt herself drowning. It was too late to return to the surface. Her head began to spin, and eventually, everything faded to black.

As she began to regain consciousness, Akinyi could feel the ground beneath her and the warm sunshine on her body. Despite the warm environment, her body was freezing as she coughed and gasped for air.

As she continued to struggle for breath, a mysterious, groggily male voice asked, "Are you alright?"

Akinyi cringed. This must be one of the king's guards. She was caught. She did not speak. When Akinyi didn't respond to the question, she suddenly felt something hit her very hard in the chest. In response to the impact, she coughed up all of the water blocking her lungs. As water flowed from her mouth, Akinyi found the strength to roll onto her right side opening her eyes. When she did, she felt the sharp sting of the bright sunlight.

The princess used her left hand as a shield against the light giving her eyes time to adjust. A few minutes passed, as her breathing calmed and returned to normal, so did her vision. She sat up slowly. Once upright, Akinyi realized that she was sitting at the edge of the lake. She massaged her temples as she tried to remember what happened and what she would tell the King when she was delivered to him.

The princess looked around to see who had saved her from drowning, but she did not see anyone. Was she dreaming? She was sure that she nearly drowned. Slowly she rose to her feet, looking all around for some sign of her savior. Finally, she concluded that whoever saved her must have run away.

Why did the person who saved me run away? Maybe he recognized me and got scared that my fiancé would see them. She reached down and grabbed her skirt and started to ring water from it as she looked around, ever mindful of the threat of being captured.

What possessed me to take the ball out of its hiding place? No, I should be happy I did that. The ball may no longer be in my possession, but King Ofori won't get his hands on it either.

She decided to head back into the palace when she heard a gargled voice ask "Your Highness, are you sure you're well enough to be walking around?"

The princess's heart skipped a beat from the shock of suddenly hearing the voice of the person who saved her. She looked all around, and once again she saw no one, making her believe that she may be losing her mind.

Just then, the gargled voice said, "I'm down here your highness."

Confused, she looked down, but the only thing she saw was a frog. The frog had large red eyes, green skin with yellow, and blue streaks on the sides of its legs that stretched down the amphibian's legs connected to four orange spongy webbed feet.

Frustrated Akinyi said, "I really have gone crazy."

The frog suddenly croaked so loud it hurt the princess' ears. The sound made her heart jump and her ears hurt. As the beating within her chest slowly calmed down, she rubbed her ears to help alleviate the pain from the loud noise. After a moment, she looked back in the frog's direction while wondering how any frog could be that nosey.

The frog stared back at her and said, "Please forgive me, I did not mean to be so loud."

Akinyi stared at the frog intensely wondering if she just saw and heard what she thought she did.

The frog stared back with a curious look on its face.

Until it finally asked, "Why are we staring at each other?"

Akinyi was frozen where she stood. Suddenly, she ran.

The frog hopped after her, shouting, "Please wait. I don't mean you any harm!"

Akinyi stopped running without turning around and cried, "Get away from me demon!"

"I'm not a demon, my lady. I'm just a simple frog."

"Liar. Frogs do not talk."

"I said I am a simple frog, not an ordinary frog."

"Just stay away from—" As she backed away from the frog, Akinyi suddenly tripped over a small rock.

When she hit the ground with a hard thud her entire body felt a searing pain from the impact. As she quickly sat up the frog jumped in front of her. The princess's body trembled as she stared at the frog in a total state of panic.

The frog looked the princess in the eyes as he said, "I'm so sorry I frightened you. I promise I mean you no harm. Did you get hurt when you fell?"

The princess shook her head, signaling no, then slowly stood up without taking her eyes off the amphibian.

The frog continued, "That's really good. Now please don't run away again. My name is Tumelo, and I would like to make a deal with you."

"I'm not making a deal with a demon."

"Once again, my lady, I am a frog, not a demon. But back to the matter at hand, I saw you dive in the lake to get a ball. I'm willing to swim down to the bottom of the lake and, get it back for you, but in exchange, I need for you to do a few things for me."

Akinyi thought *Frogs can't talk. Maybe I am having some kind of delayed reaction from that awful tea the doctor prescribed for me. I thought it was out of my system, but clearly, something is not right in my head. Yet at the same time, she wondered should I accept his offer to retrieve the ball? No, leave it at the bottom of the lake. Never forget I may not have it, but neither will the king.*

he stood up and said, "I don't know what kind of hallucination or demonic trick is going on, but I have no interest in it."

As she turned to walk away as the frog said, "You nearly killed yourself for that ball. Are you sure that you can just walk away from it?"

Akinyi stopped in her tracks, then turned and looked down at the frog. *With the king desperate to get his hands on it, that ball must be a hell of a lot more special than I thought. Should I really trust this frog.* She

41

looked to see if anyone had walked outside then looked back out at the lake. *Something inside me just knows I need that ball.*

She asked, "How can I be sure you can get my ball back for me?"

"If I can save you from drowning, I think I can get a ball out of a lake."

In a shocked tone, the princess replied, "You were the one who saved me?"

"Do you see anyone else around? Better yet you already know I am not an everyday frog, and it's not just because I told you that."

"If you saved me why not just demand what you want as a reward?"

"I respect life, and demanding something in exchange for saving it makes me feel like I am treating the value of a person as if it's not that important."

"You make a good point, and I should have said this sooner, but thank you for saving me."

"You're welcome. Now back to the matter of your ball."

"You don't waste time, do you?"

"That's because I'm hoping you accept my proposal."

"Alright, what do you want?"

"There are only three favors I want in exchange for getting you that gold ball."

"You want three favors in exchange for a single gold ball? That's rather bold."

"Seeing how important that ball is to you, I think I am in a very good position to be bold."

"Alright fine. What do you want?"

"I don't like living in this cold lake, dining on nasty bugs or sleeping on lily pads. So, I want to come and live in your palace. Secondly, I want to eat hot meals at your royal table, and finally, I want to sleep in a soft bed."

"You live in the lake."

"I'm a frog."

"I know, but you look like a tree frog. Wouldn't you be happier living out your days on a tree?"

"The trees are a worse place to live than the lake."

"Why?"

"We have established more than once I am not a normal frog. Therefore, it should be self-evident that I would be unhappy living the life of an ordinary frog, whether in a tree or a lake."

"You make a good point. I need to stop trying to loop you in with everyday frogs. But I must warn you that at this time my home is under the control of an evil man who would kill you for no reason at all."

"I am well aware you are dealing with a tyrant. But I would rather deal with him than have to spend another moment at the lake."

"Is living at the lake that bad?"

"Yes."

Akinyi thought, *I still don't trust this frog. What if I make a few demands of my own? If he agrees to them then I will be able to keep certain secrets from him to protect my interest.*

The princess took a breath then said, "Alright, Tumelo, we will only have a deal if you accept my terms."

"I'll accept whatever terms you give if it means not being at the lake anymore."

"Firstly, because of the tyrant running my house, it is going to be up to you to stay out of sight."

"He would hurt an innocent frog?"

"I have a sick feeling you're not that innocent, and I did just tell you he would kill you for the hell of it."

"That's fine with me."

"Secondly, you are not allowed in my room when I am bathing or changing my clothes."

"You don't have to worry about me being a peeper. I always respect the privacy of others."

"Good. Next, you're not allowed in my bed."

"I was not planning on getting in your bed."

"When you asked to sleep in a soft bed, I assumed you realized the only bed I could offer you was mine."

"Alright, that's fair. Instead, why don't you let me sleep on your softest pillow?"

"Fine. The next thing is that you find your way into the palace, and don't follow me when I go back inside."

The frog thought for a moment before finally saying, "Ok, I will find my own way in and not follow you."

"Finally, you must never betray me by repeating anything that you hear while living in my room."

"I have never been inclined toward snitching." The frog looked at her and asked, "Do we have a deal, or do you want something else?"

Akinyi thought for a moment before finally forcing herself to say "Fine. We have a deal."

The Frog smiled, and Akinyi was taken aback by how bizarre a smiling frog looked. There is something strange about his smile. *Maybe it just seems that way because frogs are not supposed to smile. What the hell am I thinking? The whole situation is bizarre.*

"Your Highness, I will return momentarily."

The frog then quickly hopped toward the lake. Once he reached the edge of the lake, he stared at the water intensely. Wondering if something was wrong, the princess walked over to the frog stating, "It's alright for you to reconsider."

The frog looked back at her and replied, "I'm not rethinking my decision. I just want to take in the moment of knowing that after this, I will never have to live in this nasty lake ever again."

With that, the frog jumped into the murky water and quickly disappeared.

Akinyi scanned the perimeter for guards, but still, no soldiers were milling around the garden or lake. She wondered what could be going on. *Where have all the guards disappeared to? Did the king have them all searching the palace for the golden ball?* Just in case, she found a tree and sat down, hiding from the view of anyone walking around the palace.

I hope that frog can get my ball back. If he does, do I really want to live with a slimy frog? Who knows… He may be a good spy? He is small, after all, and can easily hide.

Ten minutes passed, and the princess started to worry if something happened to the frog. She reminded herself that the lake was very deep, so obviously it was going to take him a while to get back.

As more time passed, Akinyi became worried that something had gone wrong. She feared that she would never see the ball or the frog again. The princess told herself to ignore her fears, but as more and more time went by, she started to give in. After a long while, she decided to give up and head back inside before the guards come back.

As she stood, she felt something touch the back of her foot. When she looked down to see what it was, her eyes welled up with tears of pure joy to see her gold ball. The strange symbols had disappeared, and the surface was once again smooth. As she reached for the ball, the frog jumped out of nowhere and landed on top of it.

He smiled at her while saying, "Well, princess, how did I do?"

"Wonderfully! But the ball has always been so heavy that I can't carry it back to the palace."

"Don't worry princess lift the ball you will find it easy to carry."

She lifted the ball it was light and easy to carry.

She asked, "Are you sure this is my ball? I will throw you out of the palace if I find out that you have tricked me."

"Trust me, Your Highness it is your ball."

She looked at the frog and said, "I don't have time to talk now. We can talk about this after you join me in my room."

"Which room is yours?"

"The eighth balcony on the second floor"

She pointed, "See there on the right."

The frog hopped off the ball. The princess picked it up and started to race back to her room. She decided not to reenter the palace through her mother's reading room, deciding that it may be wiser to use a secret passage instead. One of the greatest things about growing up in a palace for her was that there were tons of secret passageways, and Akinyi made it her business to know everyone.

Chapter 9

The Conversation

When she got to the palace, Akinyi walked to a spot just behind a group of pink rose bushes. She pushed a small bolder to the side, the wall opened, and Akinyi stepped into the space. She walked down the dark passageway until she reached a ladder. Holding the ball with one hand, she climbed one step at a time until she reached the top. She gently pushed the trap door a little at a time peeping out to make sure no one was in the small storage room. She rolled the ball out then pulled herself up. She closed the door, reclaimed the ball, and walked to the door that led to the hallway.

To her dismay, she saw two women talking with General Opoku in the hall. Both women had dark brown skin. One was wearing what appeared to be a very old pink dress; the neckline was so low cut that it was amazing that her nipples were covered.

The other woman might as well have been completely nude; her dress was made of white lace, so thin that it left nothing to the imagination. The three of them continued to chat until General Opoku grabbed the woman wearing the lace by her bottom as he pulled her closer to himself.

She giggled in response while the other woman watched as they exchanged a deep kiss. The other woman wrinkled her nose in seeming disgust. She reached out hugging the general's arm, saying, "Wouldn't you rather play with me?"

Growing impatient, Akinyi thought, *just take both of these whores to your room and get out of my way.* She had been gone for quite a while and feared the return of the guards to their regular patrols. To the princess surprise, General Opoku pushed the woman in the pink dress away with such force that she fell to the floor.

The woman in the white lace looked down at the other woman with a smirk of victory on her face. As she hugged the general, she said, "That's what you get for praising that spoiled little bitch." As she chastised the woman still lying on the ground, Akinyi noticed the woman dressed in white had a strange eye color. One eye was blue and the other pink.

Akinyi, taken aback, thought, *"What the hell?"*

As the woman on the ground adjusted herself, she began to rise and defended herself stating, "She is going to marry the king in a month. Why should I throw hate on her?"

The general replied, "Stupid bitch. She may be our future queen, but she has no real loyalty to the king."

In a slightly annoyed tone, the woman said, "I know that, but the king still picked her to be his wife. Meaning once they are married, she will have his ear in a way that no one else will."

The general stared at the woman in disbelief for a moment before asking, "How would she be able to do that when the king knows she hates him for taking her kingdom and murdering her father?"

The woman in the pink dress looked as if she wanted to smile but resisted the urge as she answered, "The king needs an heir so he will be spending a large amount of time with her every night. And depending on her skills, the princess, dumb or smart, is a woman and has use of a woman's power of influence."

The woman in the white lace grunted and said, "So?"

The woman in the pink dress folded her arms as she replied, "Dumb ass. If she can give him a son, and keep him happy in the bed, she is going to start building authority."

Both the general and the woman in the white lace started to laugh. In a calm tone, the general said, "Sparkle, you are stupid. I've met the princess on multiple occasions, and I can tell she is the biggest simpleton I have ever met. If it were not for that servant the king allows the princess to keep, she would forget to breathe."

The woman in the white lace started to laugh again while the princess rolled her eyes in disbelief.

Akinyi wondered why the general lied about having met her several times.

Sparkle replied, "You only confirmed what I just said."

The woman in the white lace scowled as she asked, "Why do you thinked that?"

Sparkle looked at the woman as if she wanted to slap her before replying, "Did you just say thinked? Dammit, Kitten, you want to make fun of the princess when you get dumber by the day."

"I ain't stupid's."

"Kitten, when you're referring to yourself … Never mind. I'm not going to waste time correcting you."

Sparkle turned to leave. As she walked down the hall, Kitten passionately kissed the general. Akinyi felt an uncomfortable tingling running up and down both her arms as she became more desperate for the general and the obvious prostitute to go somewhere else. *He wants to have sex with her, so why won't he just take her somewhere so they can do their business. Crap! I hope they are not planning to do it in the hallway.*

Her worst fears seemed to be coming true as the general began kissing Kitten and fondling her breasts. Akinyi could see Kitten's face clearly from where she was standing. She smiled as she saw that the bored expression on Kitten's face did not match the passionate sounds that were coming from her mouth.

She moaned, "Oh general my big strong man. Take me. I can't wait to feel your power deep inside me."

Her hands rubbing his penis through his pants. Just as she unfastened his belt, King Ofori's voice shouted, "General Opoku, what the fuck are you doing?"

For once in her life, Akinyi was happy to see her fiancé. The general quickly let go of Kitten and started to refashion his belt.

In a slightly panicked voice, General Opoku replied, "My King, I thought you were busy with combat training."

In a frustrated voice, King Ofori said, "I was, and now I'm finished. Explain to me why you are busy trying to get your dick wet instead of doing what I told you to do."

The general told Kitten to leave, but the king told her to stay. As Kitten stood looking as if she was oblivious to what was going on, while King Ofori demanded the general answer his question.

General Opoku said, "A few of the men found critical info to the location of the item in the former king of Enwayo's office. Right now, I am having my men look through it for clues."

Upon hearing that, Akinyi's heart started to race. *How can that be true when grandma told me my father knew nothing about the ball? Why did she lie? Wait, why did Papa never mention the ball if he had a book about it? Did he even know I had it?*

The king said, "I want this book brought to my quarters when your men are done looking through it."

"Yes, My King."

"Also, since you have nothing to do, I want you to ride out to the Metzin Forest."

"Why?"

50

"There is an old General there who double-crossed the former royal family. He supposedly has over six hundred men following him, and the former king was never able to successfully capture him or any of his men. I want you to see if he is willing to swear loyalty to me."

"And if he's not?"

"After we acquire the item, he will be made to regret it if he doesn't."

"I understand."

"Good."

The king then turned his attention to Kitten. He walked over to her squeezed her butt then picked her up like a doll. She giggled as he tossed her over his shoulder while saying, "You should be able to tide me over for a little while."

As he carried her off, Kitten smiled and waved goodbye to the general as she and the king disappeared down the hallway.

The general visibly upset, left in a full state of arousal, adjusted his pants as he complained that he should have taken Kitten somewhere private. Akinyi could not have agreed more. He continued to stand in the hall for a minute before finally leaving.

Once he was gone, the princess quickly checked to see if anyone else was in the hall. When she was sure no one was around, Akinyi raced over to the stairs. After making her way to the top of the staircase and making sure no one was around, she raced to her room. As she entered, she quickly closed the door behind her. Akinyi hurried to find a towel to wipe off the ball. She rushed to her wardrobe, set the ball down. Removing a clean towel, she rubbed the ball until it was once again clean and sparkling. Then another odd thing happened. She could no longer lift the ball. It had returned to its former heavyweight, so she was forced to roll it across the room to its hiding place. Once the ball was secure, Akinyi stood up and walked over to her couch.

As she was about to sit, she realized that her clothes were wet. Again, she walked to her wardrobe, opened it, and collected a robe. She walked into her bathing room, removed her clothes, and put on the robe. She pulled the drawstring bell that would summon Delu. She wanted a warm bath. She needed to think and relax, and because her fiancé was engaged, she did not have to worry about another surprise visit from him. Walking back into her bedroom, she found herself pacing back and forth until Delu came into the room.

"Yes, Princess, you called,"

"I did, Delu. Would you ask the maids to bring water? I want to take another bath before dinner."

"Yes, Princess, right away."

As she was walking out the door, Delu turned to Akinyi and said, "Maybe that crazy shit the doctor came up with is working. I will tell the cook that you are looking forward to dinner."

With that, she closed the door. Akinyi thought *I was thinking of the frog.* She had promised him food. As she thought about the frog, shock and disbelief filled her mind. *I just spent the afternoon talking to a fucking frog.* As she was wrapping her head around the events at the lake Akinyi walked over to a table against a corner wall where she opened a carafe filled with wine. The princess reached for a goblet and poured. Akinyi thought to herself, *after the day I have had, I need this.*

She took a drink. *Talking frogs,* as Akinyi finished her thought. She heard a knock at her door, Delu voice came from the other side, "Princess, may we come in?"

Akinyi answered, "Yes."

Delu entered the room, followed by six maids carrying six large buckets of water on their heads. Another maid was carrying a new

52

bowl and pitcher which she placed on Akinyi's nightstand as the other six walked into the bathing room and emptied their buckets into the princess copper tub.

After they emptied their buckets, they walked back into the princess bedroom and bowed, awaiting further instruction. She thanked them and dismissed them to go back to their other duties. The one thing that her mother and grandmother agreed on and that they both emphasized to Akinyi was to always show her servants gratitude for their efforts no matter how inconsequential the task.

As Akinyi walked into the bathing room, she saw Delu pouring lavender bath salt into the water in the tub; Delu had already placed a towel and clean bathrobe on the chair next to the tub and a washcloth on the side of the tub.

Akinyi sat her cup of wine on the chair next to the towel, removed her robe, and handed it to Delu as she climbed into the tub. The water was perfect, and the scent of the lavender was just what she needed to calm her nerves.

In a soft yet accusatory tone, Delu asked, "So, what has my princess been up to this long afternoon?"

"Up to? Delu, there isn't much that I can be up to confined in this room."

"Amazingly, it did not rain yet your clothes are soaking wet."

Delu bent over and wrapped the wet garments inside of the robe that Akinyi had just handed her and announced, "I will wash these myself. Enjoy your bath. The maids and I will return with your dinner. Then you and I can talk. There have been some new developments that you need to be aware of."

"Delu," Akinyi spoke, "I hope you know how grateful I am to you for all that you do for me."

Delu smiled bowed and left the room.

Akinyi felt awful not being able to share the events of the day with Delu. After seeing the strange symbols appear, how it changed its shape, she wondered if it could have deliberately rolled into the lake? *Did that talking frog have some connection with the ball? What do those symbols mean? What did her father know about the ball? Did he tell her brother about it? Why did her grandmother tell her that her father knew nothing about it?*

The princess reached for her wine, took a large swallow. She felt that warm filling she always got from drinking wine. Akinyi closed her eyes and laid back in the tub, took another sip of wine, and told herself to relax, that she could think about these things later.

She woke suddenly, hearing Delu's voice. "Wake up, Princess." Akinyi opened her eyes feeling more relaxed than she had in a long time. She stretched her arms. Grateful that the water was still warm Akinyi cleaned herself quickly, dried off, and put on the warm soft robe that Delu had laid out for her. Delu was waiting in her bedroom, sitting in the chair next to the sofa.

She spoke frankly, "Ok, talk to me. What have you been up to? Why were your clothes soaked?"

Akinyi remembered her grandmother's words. *Under no circumstances are you to ever tell anyone about this ball. Not even the people you trust. Promise me, Akinyi, it is more important than you realize.* Akinyi could feel her teeth start to grind. *Dammit! If I am supposed to protect the damn thing, why didn't grandmother explain the significance of the ball?* Guilt rose inside her and all the good relaxed feeling she had when she walked into the room disappeared. She knew that she had to tell Delu something

"Nothing happened." *Other than I almost died trying to save the gold ball that I can't t tell you that I have. Then I met a talking devil frog who is moving into my room if he's real.* "I snuck out and overheard a conversation between General Opoku and the King."

54

"You what? Princess, that was dangerous. What if you had been seen by one of the guards or worse by the King himself?"

"I know, but I can't just sit here all day waiting for things to happen. I heard the General say that they found a book about the gold ball in my father's room."

Delu remarked, "That is a good piece of information."

As Akinyi said, "That's not all," there was a knock at the door.

Delu rose. "It must be the maids here to clean your room." She opened the door, and the same contingent of maids that had earlier filled her tub entered the room with empty buckets and cleaning materials.

Chapter 10

Where is Tumelo?

The princess went outside to lay on the sofa on her balcony so that they could clean. Until her captivity, she had never seen the maids cleaning her room. It had always been done when she was out and about living her life. Regaining the freedom to move about as she pleased would be the only good result of her marriage to the King.

She prayed that her brother and cousin would rescue her before that dreaded day. A cool breeze and the shade from the large trees that surrounded both sides of her balcony made her stay pleasant. *It has been hours since I last saw that frog. Now is not the time for him to show up. Still, he should have arrived by now.* Two of the maids came onto the balcony, carrying bath water from her tub. They used it to water the plants in the huge flowerpots on the balcony and returned several times, watering all the flowers recycling her bathwater.

When their work was done, Delu came to the balcony door and announced, "Princess, you may return."

She bowed deeply, and they both laughed. When she entered her room, the lanterns on her night tables were lit, lanterns on all the tables were lit, adding a warm welcoming glow to the room.

When Delu left the room, Akinyi, still dressed in her robe, remembered that she was expecting her new roommate to arrive. She walked over to the wardrobe, changed from her robe into a bright red dress. Returning to the table, she placed one of the rice balls into the center of one of the bowls of palm soup and placed it opposite to her place at the table. The princess covered the bowl of soup to keep it warm. Akinyi then reclaimed her seat at the table. She was beginning to worry. *Where is Tumelo?* The idea of him being a hallucination re-entered her mind.

She looked down at her bowl of soup; it did look and smell wonderful. Despite her lack of appetite, she decided to force herself to eat. She placed the second rice ball into the center of her bowl and began to eat. Determined to fight the sensation that made eating such a punishing task, the princess picked up the spoon. Akinyi drank all of the broth and devoured about a quarter of the rice ball. Determined to finish the entire meal, she scooped up some of the meat from the bottom of the bowl, placed it in her mouth, and began to chew.

As she did, she heard Tumelo's now familiar voice say, "Dinner smells delicious. I love palm soup."

Akinyi jumped the moment she heard his voice before noticing he was sitting on top of the table.

After a moment, she responded, "I was starting to think you were never going to show up."

"I had a really hard time getting here. Several of the king's men made a game out of trying to step on me."

Akinyi frowned, "I'm not surprised all of those bastards really like killing. If I had not made a deal with their king, they would have randomly killed, raped, and robbed hundreds of my subjects for fun."

They sat in silence for a moment.

Tumelo broke the silence by asking, "Um, so roomie, was I right? Are we having palm soup for dinner?"

"Roomie?"

"I heard someone use that term once and I thought it sounded like an appropriate title for our situation."

"Oh, interesting... It is roomie."

She then pointed at the second bowl of palm soup while saying, "Your dinner is right there."

Tumelo hopped over to the bowl and smiled as he said again, "I love palm soup."

"You are a strange frog."

"Considering I can talk, you really shouldn't find anything I do weird at this point."

"I know. You're just the first talking frog who has ever moved into my room. It's going to take a bit of adjusting for me to accept that all of this is real."

"I understand. It took me a while to accept the whole frog thing too."

"What do you mean by that?"

The frog seemed to not have heard the princess' question as he stared down into the bowl of soup.

At first, Akinyi thought he was going to start eating, but instead, he looked at her and asked, "Have you already eaten?"

"I forced some food down."

Tumelo hopped over to her bowl, looked at it then looked at her, and asked, "Forgive me if I'm being too personal, but is eating a challenge for you?"

"It has become a difficult task for me these past few months. Having a sadist take over one's kingdom can do that."

Akinyi insisted, "Eat your food. You were late, and your soup is getting cold"

She handed Tumelo a teaspoon. To her amazement and delight, he ate every drop of the soup and every morsel of the rice ball.

When he finished, she commented, "You truly do love palm soup."

Tumelo burped loudly and replied, "Yes, my compliments to your cook. The meal was delightful."

They both laughed.

Chapter 11

How It All Began

As their laughter ended, Tumelo looked at Akinyi and asked "How did King Ofori gain control of your kingdom?"

"Trickery! Ofori had conquered all of the surrounding countries, including Bachtofo. Bachtofo was our neighbor to the east a country that my kingdom had been at war with for decades. My father and our people had grown weary of war, so when King Ofori offered to parlay with father with the hope of signing a peace agreement, Father jumped at the opportunity. Ofori set up a day, time, and location for the meeting.

However, when my father arrived, he was murdered along with his staff and top advisors. In a letter, Ofori claimed to know nothing about Father's murder. He said that he and his Generals did not arrive until after my father and our delegation had been killed by some unknown assailant. However, unknown to Ofori, one of my father's staff escaped the massacre, made his way back to Enwayo, and related the true events.

Ofori greeted father, and our delegation offered them drinks and a seat at the negotiating table where they all sat. Ofori then walked behind Father, pulled out a knife, and slit my father's throat. After that, the generals took out their weapons and killed almost every member of our team."

Tumelo asked, "Who survived?"

Akinyi wiping her eyes said, "My father's secretary Bondu. He was not in the room at the time. Father had sent him to fetch some paperwork. As he was returning, he heard the commotion and decided to hide until he was sure of what was happening. By the time he was able to return home and inform my brother Tuma of the events, Ofori and his forces were already invading Enwayo's northern border towns. Tuma gathered our forces as quickly as possible, but it was already too late. You see, our top military generals were all killed in the massacre. Tuma is a brave soldier, but he has very little experience fighting against a warrior like Ofori. Within a month, our forces were defeated."

In a brave and somewhat boisterous tone, she added, "Hope is not lost, though. Tuma is, as we speak, attempting to gather our allies to recapture our kingdom."

Oddly, Akinyi felt that some of the constant tension that she felt had eased after relating her story to Tumelo. She thought within herself that having a roomie might be a good thing after all.

She said, "Alright, enough about me tell me about yourself. How exactly does a frog learn to talk?"

"There is nothing really to tell."

"You're a talking frog, and I'm sure that's an interesting story."

"To sum it up, life as a frog is cold and lonely."

"Do you not get along with the other amphibians?"

"I can only communicate with humans. You're not the first human I ever spoke to."

"Really?"

"Yep. You're just the first person outside of my nation I ever spoke to who didn't think I was a demon and then tried to kill me."

"What are you talking about? I did, and still do think you're a demon."

"Princess, I am not a demon, and you at least did not try to beat me to death with a rock."

61

"If you're not some demonic frog, how come you can talk and eat human food? Along with all the other weird stuff you have been doing."

"I'm a sorcerer."

Akinyi took a quick breath, "Did you place a spell on my ball? Was that why the ball was light enough for me to carry? Was that how you got it out of the lake?"

Tumelo answered, "yes."

Instinctively, Akinyi said, "Thank you. There was no way I could have recovered the ball without your help. Tumelo bowed, "You are more than welcome."

"Are there other frog sorcerers?"

"There is a good chance that I'm the only one because I was not always a frog. I used to be human until my now sister-in-law put a curse on me."

In a surprised tone, the princess replied, "You should have started with that. So, what did you do to piss your sister-in-law off so badly that she turned you into a frog?"

"My assentation into the amphibian world all started when an old woman suddenly appeared in my palace's throne room."

"You have a palace?"

"Excuse me, I should have mentioned this before, but my older brother is King of Zeteway."

"You're a prince."

"Yes."

"Um ok, I've never heard of Zeteway."

"Of course, you haven't. Most magic wielders do not like encountering people who don't have magic. So, my ancestors put a magic barrier around our kingdom to keep people who don't have magic power away."

"How does that work?"

"The spell makes it so that if someone who does not have magical powers comes near the barrier, it causes the non-magic person to feel an overwhelming sense of fear. The fear is so unnatural that people walk in another direction convinced that they encountered a devil and believing that they never return to the area."

"Interesting, you would be amazed what fear can do."

"No, I wouldn't, my home has been invaded by a sadist."

"Fair point. Anyway, during the celebration, the night my brother ascended the throne, there was a terrible storm outside, and an old woman somehow teleported into the throne room."

"That's not something people with magic should ever do."

"Her powers were superior because centuries ago a powerful spell was cast so magic wielders could not teleport into the palace. No one had ever been strong enough to break this spell before. So, when the woman appeared, she was soaked to the bone from the storm, holding a ratty dread rose. She immediately offered the rose to my brother and me in exchange for allowing her to stay the night. I was disgusted by her having the nerve to break in and expect us to accept garbage to let her stay. Angrily, I snatched the rose from her, threw it across the room before calling the guards to take her to the dungeons. But just as quickly as I gave the order, my brother told the guards to halt.

He then asked the woman to forgive my rudeness and offered her a bed in the servant's quarters. The woman thanked my brother, and then before anyone could blink, she transformed into a beautiful sorceress. It turned out everything she had done was a test."

"What kind of test?"

"One meant to test the hearts of the royal family. Because my brother was kind to her, he was allowed to take her as his wife, and as for me, you can guess what happened."

Akinyi thought for a moment before saying, "So you were punished because you were not nice to a stranger who broke into your home."

"Yes."

"That's terrible."

Tumelo said, "Can we talk more about this later? It has been a trying day. I want to get some sleep."

"Alright let me get you a pillow."

Akinyi walked to her bed, with Tumelo hopping behind her. Once there, she grabbed the crimson red pillow that was lying between the pillows that separated the sides of her bed. She then bent down inviting Tumelo to hop on. Carrying the pillow with Tumelo on it she walked across the room, placed the pillow in the corner of her couch saying, "goodnight."

He thanked her and instantly fell asleep.

Akinyi watched him rest for a little bit before she went to grab a white nightgown, changed her clothes behind the curtain in her bathing room. After that, she climbed into her bed and fell into a deep restful sleep.

Chapter 12

The Strange Device

Akinyi opened her eyes as the morning sun crept into her bedroom. She lay in bed, stretching her arms and pulled into an upright position. Looking across the room in the direction of her couch, she observed Tumelo still sleeping deeply. *Alright, he's real. As if my life were not complicated enough.*

Losing herself in thought, she returned to a lying position, staring at the ceiling. *He said he is an actual wizard. I wonder if he might be able to use his powers to get rid of King Ofori. No, no, no, I don't know what he would want in exchange, and it may cost too high of a price.*

She decided to get out of bed. Normally, she would ring the bell for Delu and the maids to help her get ready to greet the day. But she decided to wait a little longer to allow Tumelo to wake up on his own. She felt sorry for him. He was truly enjoying his rest.

Slowly, she climbed out of bed, put on her robe, and noticed that the two bowls of soup were still on the table. She was grateful that none of the servants had retrieved the bowls. Had they come into the room, one of them might have seen Tumelo. *How am I going to be able to keep him a secret? Should I tell Delu that somehow, I have taken in a talking frog?* She sighs, there was no point in worrying about it.

Akinyi was shocked when her door flew open, and Agyapong followed by Gyasi rushed inside her room. Both men looked as if they had not slept for days.

Gyasi looked at the table for a moment before looking at the princess and asking, "Who did you eat with?"

Akinyi replied, "I had dinner with myself and what are you doing here? Have you forgotten the deal? We agreed that you would stop coming to check on me and in return, I won't tell your king that Agyapong tried to kill my friend while you watched."

"Don't try to change the subject now. Explain why there are two bowls here."

"My appetite came back, and I wanted extra food."

"Dammit woman, I'm not falling for that lie. Tell the truth before I alert the king that you snuck someone in here."

"Why do you find what I said so hard to believe?"

"If you weren't eating properly, we would have noticed."

What kind of crap is this? A blind monkey can tell that I have lost at least 20 pounds unless he is trying to set me up.

The princess asked, "What is this really about?"

"Are you that dumb I just told you to tell me who the fuck was in here last night?"

"I already told you no one was here, but since you are determined not to believe me, have the king come here. Since neither of you are willing to hold up your end of the deal, I'm going to tell him what happened yesterday. That is unless you two are willing to be smart and leave now."

Gyasi looked at the princess dumbfounded as Agyapong said, "Bold words, princess. But bold words won't save you from the king's wrath. However, we might turn a blind eye to all of this if you tell us something we want to know."

Akinyi folded her arms as she replied "What do you want to know?"

"Tell us where the gold ball is."

66

The princess looked both men in the eyes as she replied, "What are you talking about?"

In a pissed off tone, Agyapong replied, "Bitch, stop lying and tell us what we need to know."

"How can I tell you something I don't know?"

The door opened, and Delu walked in with a tray holding the same teapot and pink teacup from the day before.

She seemed to read the room before asking, "What's going on?"

Akinyi frowned as she said, "Nothing. These two are leaving, and they are not coming back."

The two men looked at the princess for a moment before turning and walking out of the room, slamming the door as they left.

Delu put the tray on the table as she asked the princess, "What just happened?"

Akinyi explained what had just occurred as Delu poured a cup of what Akinyi feared was the doctor's concoction.

Akinyi flinched at the memory of its awful taste as she replied, "I'm not surprised."

The princess looked in the direction of Tumelo's pillow wondering what she was going to tell Delu, but he had disappeared. She wondered where he went but decided not to worry about it because she was not comfortable with Delu encountering Tumelo just yet.

Delu handed her the cup, and the princess asked, "You're not trying to give me more of that nasty tea, are you?"

"No, this is hot pineapple juice with ginger. Even though that gray mess helped you want food again, the doctor wants you to start drinking hot pineapple juice with ginger every morning to help supplement your meals."

Akinyi started to drink the juice, and the moment the liquid went down her throat, she felt her stomach growl for the first time in a long time. As she wondered why her will to eat was back so suddenly.

Delu said, "That moron did not collect your bowls last night."

"Who are you talking about?"

"This new girl named Honey. The usurper brought her into the servants' quarters last night and told the head of the staff that she was going to be one of your maids. I think that is a dumb way to plant a spy. But it made it easier for all of us to know she is a spy, so I won't complain."

"How are you so sure that she is a spy?"

"It's been over two months since he has taken over the kingdom and he has never once made any additions or changes to the staff. Then he suddenly drops some woman who is foul-mouthed and bad at basic tasks to be a maid. She's the reason I have not been able to sneak off as much to try and steal that book."

"Technically, the book was my father's. And since my father is no more, it belongs to me now, so you're just recovering stolen property."

Delu smiled, "Semantics aside, do you find it strange he made this woman a maid at the same time we discovered he is desperate to get ahold of that gold ball?"

"I see your point, but the usurper does not know that we know that he is looking for the ball. So there may be another reason he did it."

"If there is another reason, he went out of his way to personally make that woman a maid, you might be about to find out."

Delu pointed in the direction of the secret entrance to the Akinyi's room, and they saw Owusu walk in.

Seeing him made Akinyi's heart race. She wanted nothing more than to run into his arms. But she could not risk reopening her romance with Owusu. She reminded herself not to get too close to him. She put her cup on the table as Delu quickly excused herself.

When Delu was gone, Akinyi looked at Owusu and asked, "What are you doing here? You know coming here is dangerous? Delu just told me that the King had planted a spy to act as one of my maids."

"I used our secret passageway to enter the palace. I wanted to share with Delu some new information that I have just discovered. Then I decided that it is important for you to hear what I have to say."

Akinyi walked to her sofa, picked up the red pillow, now Tumelo's bed, and sat it on the table in front of the sofa. Owusu walked across the room and sat next to her on the sofa. When he sat down, Akinyi could feel her temperature rising. The princess told herself to keep her cool so he would not notice.

She asked, "Owusu, have you any information about the new maid and why after all this time the King decide to plant a spy in my household staff?"

"Delu only told me about the new maid this morning. I haven't had time to gather any information about her: where she came from or what the usurper intends for her to do. Shortly after Delu shared information with me about the King's search for this golden ball, I stumbled across some valuable information. My contacts told me King Ofori's army is very weak."

The princess felt as if someone punched her in the gut. Quickly she replied "Impossible! A weak army could not have conquered this kingdom, nor any of the other nations under King Ofori's control."

Owusu continued, "At first I thought the same thing. Then I considered Ofori has a limited number of men. Sure, he forces male captives to serve in his military. But many of them run away when the opportunity arises. So, he has to leave a fair amount of his men behind to maintain his new territories. Leaving his army overstretched.

But that still leaves the question of how he can hold on to his new territories? While making plans to take over more nations. When I discovered the answer, I learned that Ofori's victories are all due to some strange device. He discovered a few years after ascending to the throne of his home country."

In a questioning tone, Akinyi repeated, "A device, what kind of strange device can make an army more powerful?"

"This device makes his soldiers impervious to pain and gives them superhuman strength."

Akinyi interrupted, "That would explain why Agyapong did not react when I slashed his arm?"

Owusu spoke, "What are you talking about?"

"I thought that Delu would have told you that Agyapong tried to strangle her. In a desperate attempt to save her, I used my letter opener to slash his shoulder. I cut him deeply, yet he did not react when I did."

Owusu leaned into Akinyi, looking her in the eyes, and said, "If he strangled Delu, why did you not report the incident to the usurper?"

"I thought about it, but something told me that it would be wiser not to report it. I decided to use that bit of information to blackmail those two idiots instead."

She did not tell Owusu that the two assholes had already violated their agreement.

Instead, she said, "They are forbidden from coming into my room. No more random checking up on me at all hours of the day and night."

"Did he touch you when you slashed his arm?"

Akinyi lied, "No, he wouldn't dare"

The last thing I need is to have Owusu hunting Agyapong to seek revenge.

"And Delu is fine. We have them where we want them. That's the end of the situation."

Owusu, in a voice of acceptance, said, "Okay, I get your message. Anyway, my source told me that the device is capable of winning battles on its own. It can kill hundreds of soldiers at a time. How this is possible or whether this is true or not, I can't say. The usurper is running out of the material that powers the device. He only has enough of its initial power source to last until your wedding day. If he doesn't find more by then, taking back Enwayo will be a piece of cake."

"I don't get it, Owusu, Ofori has been tearing this palace apart looking for a gold ball. The treasury is filled with gold, why doesn't he just melt some down and fashion it into a ball? What is so special about this particular ball and why would my father have a book about a gold ball? All these questions are beginning to drive me nuts. None of it makes sense."

"I know what I said so far sounds crazy and confusing, but just hear me out. The gold ball he is looking for is not really made of gold."

Shocked Akinyi could only muster one simple word, "What?"

"It is some kind of material called emidrestor. This mineral looks like gold and has the same weight as gold, but it is something different and more valuable; it can, in fact, fuel a machine capable of winning wars. "

Akinyi and Owusu sat in silence, absorbing the information Owusu had just relayed to her. Akinyi's mind raced. *No wonder my grandmother swore me to secrecy.*

The sound of Owusu's voice brought her back to reality.

"Last night, the usurper held a meeting with some of his top officials in the council room, all who have been tasked with finding the gold ball were in attendance. I used the passageway behind the wall to spy on the meeting. The King was acting jittery, scratching his arm uncontrollably, walking back-and-forth. His eyes were darting oddly from one person to another. He gave a long ranting speech about his people not being able to follow a simple task. At one point he pounded the table shouting, 'How hard can it be to find this ball?!'

"After ranting for a while, he suddenly killed three of the people sitting at the table. He said as a lesson to the others of the seriousness of the matter. He went on and on for another twenty minutes telling them how he will tolerate no more slackers. The man is off his rocker. After dismissing everyone, he drank something from a goblet sitting on the table. After a few moments, he seemed to return to normal. He stopped scratching his arm, and his eyes seemed to return to normal. I don't know if part of his strange behavior can be a side effect of using the machine. If it gives people superhuman strength, then it may eventually affect their minds."

Akinyi asked, "Did any of the others at the table display any unusual behavior? Come to think of it, one of the women generals that he killed had her head on the table the entire time. Both men were slouched over in their chairs."

"So, from what you are telling me maybe the King's soldiers are beginning to weaken."

Akinyi thought to herself, "*Could that be why Agyapong and Gyasi looked as if they hadn't slept for days?*"

She spoke aloud, "Do you suppose that the king and his troops are beginning to physically weaken?"

"I have considered that. If it's true, it will make recapturing Enwayo a real possibility and perhaps sooner than we could ever hope. One thing I do know is that the usurper is insane, and I am concerned for your safety. We know that this man broke tradition of never killing at a negotiation and killed your father in cold blood. I feel that we must get you out of here as soon as we can make arrangements."

"Don't you see, Owusu, I can't leave now that we know about this device and more importantly about this mineral emidrestor. Other than the fact that it is rare, do you know anything else about it? Where does it come from?"

"No, Akinyi, I have learned nothing more than what I have told you."

She looked him directly in his eyes and stated, "We must make sure he does not find it first. But just as important, we have to find and destroy this machine."

"Shouldn't we try to recover it instead?"

"Owusu, we grew up in the palace. So, you know better than anyone that my brother is tired of war and only wants peace. You also know my cousin and the rest of our allies are also weary from decades of war, and they want peace as well. Sure, none of them will want to use this powerful device, but they won't destroy it either. All of them will think it is a good idea to keep it around in case another threat like the usurper immerges."

"What's wrong with that?"

"The problem is I know what my brother, cousin, and allies will do, but I don't know what their children will do. Or what their children's children will do and so on. Eventually, someone is going to come along and probably do far worse things than the usurper. What if more than one of these machines is created? Can you imagine the loss of lives and the destruction that will accompany it? We must do all that we can to prevent that day from coming."

"I understand your point, Akinyi, but I think that we should consider using the machine to help our side. We can use it to return things to the way they were before the mad King took over. Maybe then destroy it."

"Owusu, you have just told me that you believe that Ofori is insane. What if the price of using the machine is insanity or something worse that we do not yet know?"

Changing the subject, Owusu moved closer to her, touching her thigh with his hand. Akinyi's heart raced as he leaned over and gave her a deep passionate kiss. She went limp in his arms. Her body burned with desire. She found herself returning his kiss. Remembering her vow, Akinyi pushed him away.

"Owusu, stop. I told you that our romantic relationship is over. "

Owusu released her. "Akinyi, why are you pushing me away? These months without you have been pure misery for me."

"You and I both know that our relationship has no future. If in a month I am forced into marriage with Ofori, we will no longer be able to see one another. He will probably have me watched every minute of every day. Even if he is defeated, it is obvious what will happen when my brother is king. There are no fairytale endings for us, only sadness, pain, and misery. Ending it now on friendly terms, in the long run, will be easier on the both of us."

Owusu's body stiffened. "I know that you are likely right, but no one knows the future. Besides, why not live in the moment? Let tomorrow take care of itself."

Akinyi remained firm. She stood looking down into Owusu's eyes, "No, Owusu, I must live in the real world. It will destroy both of us in the long run if we continue our relationship."

Looking into his eyes, reminded Akinyi that part of the reason that she had refused to leave Enwayo with her brother was the love that she had for Owusu. She knew that if she left, they would never have seen one another again. He stood and faced her. That strength in his eyes had always made Akinyi feel safe.

"My princess, I will do as you ask, but I will never give up on us." He kissed her on the cheek. As he did so, it took all of her will not to turn her face so that their lips could once again meet.

He said, "While I am here in the palace, I will see if I can find any more information on the whereabouts of the device if it does exist, or the ball."

He walked to the secret entrance to her room, looked back at her, smiled, and left.

After Owusu left, Akinyi sat quietly thinking as she drank the now warm pineapple juice with ginger that Delu had brought her earlier. She knew she would be lying to herself if she did not admit she already really missed Owusu. Whenever he was near her even if he was aggravating his presence made her happy.

She wanted desperately for him to come back. To cuddle like they used to. The princess sighed and told herself to try to take her mind off of her tragic romance.

Akinyi knew she had a tone of more pressing issues to worry about. King Ofori, the strange weapon, the freaky talking frog living in her room and, many other things. Sitting around trying to handle her broken heart had to wait. At least that is what she told herself to help not think about the pain.

As she continued to sip her drank. She was delighted as she realized that she was enjoying its delicious flavor. Akinyi had lost a lot of weight. She was aware that none of her clothes fit her properly anymore. Her curves were disappearing as she turned into skin and bones.

Akinyi thought it was odd that during his visit to her room that the King had not noticed how thin she had become. But the comments made by Gyasi and Agyapong saying that they had not noticed that she had lost weight made her wonder if this lack of ability to notice things were a side effect of using the device. Did it give them great strength yet affect their minds? Would it eventually drive them insane? That was all she needed; a kingdom filled with brutal insane soldiers. She heard her stomach growling. Her appetite had returned.

Chapter 13

Tumelo's Past

Tumelo shocked her by suddenly jumping up onto the table. He had a big smile on his face as he said, "Good morning, princess."

Akinyi looked at the frog as she replied, "Where have you been?"

"I was scared that those two men who barged in your room earlier would try to crush me. So I snuck out onto the balcony for a while."

"I did not know I left the door open."

"You didn't. I used my powers to open it myself. That is how I got into your room last night. You're very good at going and coming into the room without anyone noticing."

"Thank you! It took me months of practice to pull that off."

"Why did you have to practice that?"

"No special reason. My brother and I used to sneak into the kitchen late at night to eat extra desserts. So, we practiced using our powers to open and close doors so that no one would hear us."

"Oh, anyway how did you sleep?"

Garnishing that strange smile of his, Tumelo answered, "I have not had a sleep that good since I was a human. Speaking of humans, I heard those scary guys screaming at you about that gold ball. Why do they want it so bad?"

"I have no idea."

Tumelo looked at her she thought somewhat skeptically and said, "Really? I thought since you were willing to risk your life for it, you would know."

The princess guessed Tumelo had not heard her conversation with Owusu. She also had no desire to tell him anything involving the ball, because she was still unsure if she could trust him.

Akinyi replied, "If you must know, that ball is only important to me because it's the last remaining good memory I have of my grandmother."

"I understand how you feel, but I don't think that ball is worth your life."

The princess was happy Tumelo seemed to believe her lie but told herself to be cautious. He may be pretending to believe her.

Then she said, "When I dove into the lake to retrieve my ball, my mind was under so much distress that I wasn't thinking clearly."

Tumelo thought for a moment, then said, "Hey princess, when do you think breakfast will be ready?"

"You're really excited about food."

"You would be too if all you've had to eat for a year and a half was bugs."

"Speaking of that, you never explained the point of the test that turned you into a frog, or why your brother banished you instead of helping you."

"Oh, right. I never finished the story…"

Akinyi interrupted, "Tell me about the test you said your nation's council of elders started. Who are the members of this council and why do they have so much authority over the royal family? In Enwayo, no one would dare to question the Kings' fitness to govern."

Tumelo began, "The council of elders consists of older wizards and witches that have mastered magic and become the most powerful wizards in the world. They have the power to deny the heir to the throne from assuming power; because it was decided long ago that just because a person is the eldest son of the king does not mean that that person is capable of being a good and wise king."

"So that is the reason for the test, but what happens if he fails?"

"Then the next in line is chosen or one of the cousins. Eventually, someone will pass the test."

"So, is your sister-in-law a member of this council of elders or in reality, some old lady transformed by magic into a beautiful young woman? You told me that she had to be very powerful to transport herself into your throne room."

Tumelo continued, "Members of the council also choose the queen. When my brother was born, all of the baby girls in the kingdom were tested to see which one possessed the strongest magic. That baby is taken from her parents and raised by the elders at a secret location. She undergoes rigorous magical training, and to round off her personality, she is also trained in the social graces. At some point, she is told that she will one day become Queen of Zeteway. But there is a catch."

Akinyi rolled her eyes as she thought, *How did I know there would be a catch?*

"No one is perfect, not even the members of the council. They realize that they may have chosen the wrong baby girl. Therefore, there is a constant search for young girls who show the potential of becoming very powerful witches. These girls are allowed to live at home with their parents. They are, however, monitored closely. When the chosen one reaches the age of ten, the council members arrange a series of tournaments. The chosen one must compete against this group of contestants. If she ever loses to a challenger, she will be killed and replaced by the winning contestant. You see she has been taught magical secrets that only royals and council members are allowed to know. Such knowledge in the wrong hands can destabilize and possibly destroy Zeteway. Needless to say, my sister-in-law learned well, and only a few, if any, can match her power."

Akinyi asked in a puzzled tone, "Your brother's ability to rule with kindness and fairness were tested which is understandable because he was to be crowned King. Why then were you turned into a frog?"

Tumelo continued, "When a new king ascends the throne, he and whoever is second in line are given a test to assess their worthiness."

"This whole thing sounds backward to me. Why weren't the two of you tested before your brother was crowned?"

"I agree, but no one in my kingdom likes change. No one challenges the council. That group of old fogies is incapable of accepting any new ideas. It has been done this way for hundreds of years and so it will remain."

"Ok. So, if this test is given at random, why then when this strange old woman appeared out of nowhere did you not recognize the possibility that this might be a test?"

"My brother and I were prepared for the test, or so I thought. Our parents had over the years given us special test of wisdom and how to cast certain spells that were the usual method that the council used for the test. As I said before, the members of the council are set in their ways. It is rare for them to deviate."

"Just your luck to be there when they decided to change, still your brother did pass."

Tumelo seemed to frown if Akinyi was reading his facial expression correctly, "If only it were that simple. You see, princess, it was only after I was turned into a truth-telling frog. Part of my curse is that I cannot lie."

Akinyi thought to herself, *why is he emphasizing the fact that he can't lie. Is it a trick? I just met him yesterday so. How am I supposed to be able to tell if he is lying or not?*

"Anyway, I learned that my shit of a brother knew about the test several weeks before it happened."

"So, the two of you weren't close? Was this his way of getting rid of you?"

In a wistful tone, Tumelo said, "I always believed that we were close. We were constant companions until I was transformed into my present state."

"Did your parents tell him? You said that over your lifetime they prepared the two of you for the test."

"No, the proud informant was my future sister-in-law. It turns out that some years earlier, she had been allowed to go to the market alone. While there, she saw a procession as my father and brother traveled to our summer palace. They got out of their carriage and walked about the market greeting our subjects."

Tumelo's tone gave Akinyi a chill as he said, "Dear sister-in-law laid eyes on my brother, fell instantly and completely in love."

Akinyi almost laughed but controlled herself, "That is a little fairy tallish, isn't it? I mean love at first sight. Was she deprived of all companionship?"

"I honestly don't know."

Akinyi spoke frankly, "You know these elders of yours may have cast a love spell on her to ensure that she and your brother would have a happy marriage."

His tone changed as he replied, "I never thought of that, but I have never heard of such a thing being done. There is also the possibility that she is not altogether mentally stable. From that day

81

forward, she was determined that nothing would interfere with her marriage to the man she loved."

Several weeks before my brother's coronation, she snuck into the palace introduced, herself to my brother, and gave him the complete lowdown of what the test would entail. The coldness returned to Tumelo's voice as he added, he said that he did not share this information with me because he was sure with my kind spirit, that I would have passed. To top things off, my brother is the King of magic. He can change me back, but he refused to do so."

There was a knock on the door. Akinyi said, "Come in."

The door opened, and Serwa came in with breakfast. She greeted Akinyi as she stared at Tumelo, good morning. Princess."

"Good morning, Serwa."

Serwa continued holding tightly to her tray as she asked, "Your highness, why is there a frog on the table?"

Akinyi looked at her as she answered, "It's my new pet."

"Okay fine, but get it off of the table, you don't want it jumping on your food."

As the princess picked up Tumelo and placed him on the floor, the servant put the tray on the table and removed the cover, revealing two large plates of sausage, bacon, toast, roasted fish, fufu, and two small bowls of peanut butter soup.

Serwa explained that the cook prepared double of everything because he figured the princess was starving now that her appetite was back. After Serwa left to attend to other duties, Tumelo hopped back onto the table and looked at his plate as if he was staring at something truly beautiful. The princess could tell that she was not going to hear any more of his story until he finished eating. She cut his meat into small pieces then scooted his food closer to him, and after quickly thanking her, Tumelo started to use his tong to eat. Akinyi then picked up her spoon and began eating as well.

82

For the first time in months, Akinyi not only enjoyed eating but she was stuffed. Akinyi was amazed at how much food he could eat. After breakfast, he excused himself to exercise, saying that he needed to work off some of the food that he had eaten.

After Tumelo hopped outside, Akinyi began to assess the details of the story he had told her. King Ofori, his strange device, the mystery of the golden ball were trouble enough for her. She wanted to believe Tumelo. It would be great to have an ally and a wizard no less, yet, she had doubts.

What was that bit about not being able to lie? Why would that be a part of the curse? Was he such a liar that he could not be trusted? Why would a brother that he claims was his closest friend betray him? Akinyi's thoughts were interrupted by the sound of tapping on her balcony doors.

The princess looked in the direction of the noise. She realized that it was a dove tapping at her door. Excitedly, she raced to the door. At last, a message. *Had Owusu or Delu found some new information? Her chest pounded, she dared not hope. Could it be from Tuma? Have the allies agreed to a plan of attack?*

When she opened the door, a brown dove flew in and landed on her table. She rushed to the table and sat down in one of the chairs reaching for the bird, and she removed the rolled-up message from its leg. She then carried the dove back to her door and released it and closed the door. After reclaiming her seat, Akinyi untied what turned out to be a three-page note. The last page was tied separately. Akinyi began to read.

Your highness, this is General Idris. His Highness Prince Tuma along with myself and the rest of our troops have arrived at King Bonsu's palace. Sadly, Prince Tuma received several injuries during our escape, but he is expected to make a full recovery in a few months. Also, even though your cousin, King Bonsu, is going to fully support the battle to retake Enwayo, many of our allies are terrified of King Ofori and refuse to help us. King Bonsu refuses to give up hope, and I'm currently attempting to help him change their minds. I am so sorry that we can do nothing to stop your marriage to that psycho. But I promise you and Enwayo will be liberated from that monster.

Knowing that the message had been sent by Idris Akinyi assumed that the part tied separately must be a special message to Delu from her husband, the princess set it aside on the table. There was more to Delu's husband's message, but the princess's eyes were too full of tears to continue reading. As she wiped her tears away she could not help smiling with joy at the knowledge that her little brother, Delu's husband, and the rest of the army were alive and safe. As she was about to continue reading, she heard a knock and Serwa voice requesting entrance, "May I come in." Akinyi quickly rolled the messages and placed them under the cushion of the chair that she was sitting in. Yes, please. Serwa, the maid who brought her breakfast earlier entered the room.

Serwa looking at the empty plates said, "Princess, everyone will be so pleased that you enjoyed your meal."

"Yes, I can truly say that I did. Tell Zumba that a few more meals like that and I will be back to my old size in no time."

Serwa smiled and collected the dishes. As she left the room, Delu rushed in. Delu and Serwa shared a passing greeting as Delu closed the door behind her.

Delu rushed over to the table and sat in the chair next to Akinyi, catching her breath, she looked at Akinyi and announced, "We found it"

"Found what?"

"We found the device."

"How did you find it?"

"One of my subordinates discovered the building that the usurper has set up as a makeshift base. After my informant alerted me, I told Owusu. Since you gave us the order to destroy it, we decided that it would be wise to get the job done immediately just in case the usurper decided to move it."

Akinyi beamed, hugging Delu "You destroyed it already."

"No, your highness, I am sorry to say that we were unsuccessful. We rode out with a team of our best people and a cart full of several containers of oil. The plan was to burn down the building, believing that in the process the fire would destroy the device. You know better than anyone that oil is a useful tool for setting fires and considering you used it several times to burn down enemy strongholds. Well, when we got to where the device is being housed, we hid the oil. Then Owusu and I decided that we should sneak inside to get an idea of how we should set things up to burn it all down. The place was under heavy guard, so naturally, it took us a while to get into the building. But once we did, my goodness, princess, that thing is unnatural. Having seen it I am not sure that even fire can destroy it."

"What does it look like?"

"I don't know if I can describe the thing. Let me say it is huge, so it's more than a little astounding none of us were aware of it. I don't even know how he managed to move it from one location to another. There was a small ball of that emidrestor stuff floating in the center of it. Surrounding the emidrestor were spikes, hundreds of spikes, constantly shifting positions."

The base is made out of some sort of grey material we were not able to get close enough to determine what material it was.

"Really? Could you tell what caused the emidrestor and these spikes to be able to float?"

"I don't know, but after seeing that thing, I feel even more certain that you were right to order us to destroy it."

Akinyi inquired, "You were so close, what stopped you from destroying the thing?"

Delu's face seemed to be filled with a mixture of concern and fear. Akinyi's heart skipped a beat. She and Delu had been through many dangerous missions and battles together over the years and through it all she had never seen fear in her friend's eyes.

Delu continued, "That is the part of the story that is the most frightening and bizarre. Just as quickly as we entered the room containing the device, Owusu and I had to escape because the men the usurper had protecting the device knew we were there. They could smell us."

"What?"

"I know that sounds crazy but no sooner did we get inside than the guards started sniffing around like dogs. At first, we were perplexed as to what they were doing. But some of them started shouting that they could smell intruders. The next thing that we knew they came rushing in the direction of where we were hiding, let us just say that the two of us were lucky that they weren't able to catch us. We managed to get back to the location where the oil and horses were stored. We had a temporary base set up, so we went there to regroup."

Akinyi a look of puzzlement on her face said, "So you said that it was as if they could smell you like guard dogs?"

In a thoughtful tone, Delu answered, "Yes, Owusu and I believe that this is one of the abilities that using the device gives the usurper's soldiers."

Akinyi responded, "Human guard dogs. Delu what kind of monstrous demons are we dealing with?"

"I don't know princess but they will not be easy to defeat unless we find a way to destroy that device."

87

They sat in silence for a few moments each thinking about the task ahead of them.

Akinyi said, "Your information sent me into such a state that I forgot that I received some great news just before you came in."

Akinyi stood and took the messages from her hiding place underneath her cushion. She handed it over to Delu. Akinyi could see Delu's eyes light up as she recognized her husbands' handwriting. Before she began to read the message Delu pulled the letter close to her body as if hugging it. She read the entire message. When she finished, she began reading the private note that General Idris had included for her eyes only. She smiled coyly as she read.

When she was done, Akinyi, in a teasing tone asked, "I'm guessing Idris misses you."

"He misses me alright, and he wants us to start a family as soon as this is over."

"What changed his mind about being a parent?"

"You know, your Highness, all of our lives, Enwayo has been at war. Idris believes that when we rid our country of the usurper, there will, at last, be peace. The idea of children sounds nice to him. I have to admit it makes me more than a little happy."

"I bet that he is reminding you of just how much fun making that baby will be."

Delu laughed, "He does not need to remind me. With a man like mine, I can't forget. I look forward to his homecoming. Don't expect to see us for a month at least."

Both women laughed. Delu said, "This is good news because we will need help destroying that device."

"I will see if Owusu can get a message through. Before our forces and our allies return, that machine must be destroyed, or they will be defeated."

Delu reread the private letter from her husband, she then rerolled it and tied it, handed it to Akinyi, and said, "Princess, will you please keep this in a safe place for me. With that Honey woman hanging around, I don't want it falling into the wrong hands. I tell you that woman is getting on my last nerve. She has taken to following me around."

"Why is she following you?"

"She knows that Owusu and I are friends. So, she thinks that she can use me to get to him."

Delu smiled as she noticed that Akinyi began to fiddle with the papers in her hand, she reached over and patted Akinyi's hand and said, "You don't have to be afraid."

Akinyi said sharply, "Afraid of what? Owusu has every right to move on. I want him to find someone else and be happy."

Using a firm tone Delu stated, "Frankly, Princess, we both know that that is a load of crap. Save that for the usurper. Owusu loves you, and you love him. Pulse I have a strong feeling that Owusu is determined to win you back."

Akinyi sighed, "Can we please talk about something other than my love life?"

"Considering we need to talk about, Honey, your love life has to be front and center."

"What does her infatuation with Owusu have to do with anything important?"

"Firstly, did he tell you he is masquerading as the head of the staff?"

"No."

"You know that Mando the former head of staff left with Prince Tuma. Honey wants to get access to your family's vault. The usurper wants to open it, and he believes that Owusu as head of the staff can access it for him."

"Why?"

"I don't know. All I found out is that he does not want you to know he wants access to it. Although I suspect it has to do with the emidrestor."

"Well, it does not matter. I do not know how to get into the vault."

"But he thinks the head of the staff does. However, since torture would violate your agreement, he put Honey in charge of finding out."

"At least he is committed to the agreement."

"That's only because you have him convinced you won't marry him if he violates your agreement."

"Wait a minute, Owusu got back yesterday, how is he able to have them think he is the head of staff."

"Simple. The head of the staff does not do a lot of work. He just makes sure everyone else is working so they can disappear and reappear easily."

"Funny, I never noticed that."

"Anyway, while Honey wastes time trying to get Owusu's attention I'm going to see if I can get ahold of that book."

"Are you talking about the book the usurper took from my father's office?"

"Yes. At first, we were not prioritizing the book because we were following your order to destroy the device. So there did not seem to be a reason to immediately worry about the book or that emidrestor the usurper is looking for. After what happened when we tried to destroy the device, I got a feeling that what we are dealing with is way out of our league."

"From what you told me, I have to agree. Even when Bonsu sends help to destroy the device, it may not be enough since we have no idea of what we are dealing with."

"I currently have one of my men watching the usurper's room. I will immediately report back once it is in our position."

"All right."

With that, Delu reached over and touched the letter from her husband and left the room. Akinyi immediately placed the messages she had received earlier under her chair cushion. She would store them in a secret hiding place once she was sure Tumelo was not around.

Chapter 15

The Price to Be Paid

Akinyi questioned the decision of allowing Delu and Owusu to endanger their lives trying to destroy the device when she had a powerful wizard living in her room. *I don't altogether trust Tumelo, so getting him involved may not be a good idea.* As she thought, Akinyi heard Tumelo croaking outside on the balcony. She wondered what he was doing.

Twenty minutes, after sunset Akinyi sat on her couch with her room bathed in candlelight while she was still debating with herself. *Tumelo is a wizard who probably has the power to solve the problem. My cousin is sending help. Why should I waste time making another deal with Tumelo? I do not even know if I can or should trust him? He did tell me that because of the curse that he is unable to lie. But it's not like I know him well enough to tell if he is lying or not. Even if he is telling the truth the price for saving my kingdom may be too high a cost. Still what Delu said about the men grading the device. What price will I have to pay if I play with magic? When Delu finds that book I can make an informed decision.*

Just as that thought crossed her mind, Tumelo entered the room. He hopped onto the coach as the princess looked at him and asked, "What have you been up to?"

"Nothing much I was just engaged in a little magic practice and hopping around to work off that magnificent lunch we enjoyed earlier. You know princess you have an excellent cook."

Akinyi smiled *you truly have a magnificent appetite.*

She said, "you were practicing magic?"

"Yeah, but I only did small spells so no one would notice. By the way, when is dinner arriving?"

"Why are you always so hungry?"

"Using magic takes a lot of energy."

The topic of magic made Akinyi think that it would not be a bad idea to at least inquire what the risk would be if Tumelo took care of her enemies. She took a deep breath before asking, "Tumelo, I have a question."

"What is it, princess?"

"Can you use magic to get rid of King Ofori and all of his soldiers?"

Tumelo stared at the princess for a moment before finally saying, "I can take life. But I do not take the action of doing so lightly. So, if you want me to end King Ofori along with all of his soldiers for you, it is going to cost you a very high price."

"What is your price?"

"You have to agree to become my wife and seal the deal with a kiss."

In a surprised tone, the princess said, "Why do you want to marry me? We don't know one another."

"How well we know each other does not matter?"

"Fair point, but you are currently an amphibian. How are we supposed to convince anyone to wed us?"

"Remember how I told you my brother refused to use his power to turn me back because it was not beneficial to him. It was because he knew he could use me to expand his kingdom."

"What do you mean?"

"There are two ways to break the curse on me. The first as you already know is to have the king of magic reverse it. However, the second option is for a princess to agree to marry me and seal the agreement with a kiss.

My brother wants to expand the reach of his kingdom to non-magic nations. But the nobility of my nation would go on a tirade if he tried to marry a non-magic wielder. Also, willingly having me marry a non-magic wielder is not an option as well."

"I don't understand your brother's logic. Having you marry a princess who has no magical power to remove your curse instead of removing it himself is still willingly having you marry a non-magic user."

"You're right about that. Luckily for him, only a select few know he can remove the spell, and they will never go against what he wants."

"I'm guessing what you're alluding to is that your banishment was nothing more than a ploy. So that he could send you off to find a desperate princess who would kiss you, then you turn back into a sorcerer prince and marry her. After that, your brother shows up so happy to see you a human once more.

Everyone will be happy and rejoice until suddenly misfortune befalls everyone who is ahead of you with any claim to the throne of your bride's kingdom. However, instead of ascending the throne yourself, you will hand power over to your loving brother."

"That's his plan in a nutshell."

"Too bad for both of you, I have no desire to play along with it. So, you're going to have to find some other princesses whose kingdom has been taken over by a tyrant to kiss you."

"Hold on, princess. If I had any plans to go through with what my brother wanted, I would not have told you what he wants to do."

"How do I know you are not using a common misdirection?"

"I cannot lie."

"How am I supposed to be sure you're being honest about that?"

"I see your point, but I don't have any desire to go through with his plan after he made me live as a frog for a year and a half just to expand his kingdom. There is nothing in his plan that would benefit me."

"Just because you told me that does not mean I believe you."

"I guess as long as we have no way to prove I can't lie, there is no convincing you. But please understand, I don't want to be a frog anymore. So, I am willing to do whatever it takes to be human again."

"Why do you specifically have to marry a princess?"

"You would have to get the person who created the curse to answer that for you I'm just a victim of their magic."

"Your sister-in-law…"

Chapter 16

Bloodshed

Suddenly, they both heard Gyasi shout, "Dammit bitch, just tell us where she is hiding the fucking thing!"

Soon after the shouting stopped, they both heard Delu scream. In response, the princess quickly rushed out of her room and into the hallway. As soon as she entered the hall, she saw Delu on her knees. Delu's right eye had come into contact with a fist from the dark circle around it.

She was holding her stomach in a way that indicated she had been punched there as well. Akinyi quickly rushed over to Delu. As she helped her up, she shot an angry look at the men.

Once Delu was on her feet, Akinyi asked, "What happened?"

Delu was shaking as she said. "I was g-going to y-y-your room to…"

"Slow down and just take a breath. Then try to tell me what else happened."

Still shaking, Delu forced herself to take a deep breath before pointing at the men and saying "They started demanding I tell them where you are hiding some golden ball. After I told them I knew nothing about this gold ball, Gyasi punched me in the face. Then I tried to get back on my feet, and Agyapong kicked me in the stomach."

The very blood within the princess' veins started to boil she shot a dirty look at the two men who were still laughing.

She shouted, "What the fuck is so damn funny?"

Agyapong chuckled as he said, "Stop being so dramatic. The little bitch was taking too long to do her job, so she had to be reprimanded."

Akinyi responded, "I already know that it's a lie. But I'll deal with you two later. Come on Delu I will help you get to the doctor."

In an authoritative tone, Gyasi said, "Hold it, princess. We were going to be pleasant about you stepping out of your room for a few minutes. But we are not about to let you run around the palace doing as you please."

The princess glared at Gyasi as she shouted, "It would be smarter for you to start running away! I turned a blind eye the first time you violated your king's orders but not this time!"

She wrapped her hand around Delu's waist to help her stand straight. The two of them started to walk slowly down the hall.

In a weak voice, Delu said, "Thank you, princess, but I can make it on my own."

Akinyi replied, "Don't be silly. You need help getting to the infirmary"

"No, even if the king punishes those two for getting out of line, he will..."

Before another word could escape Delu's lips, Agyapong plunged a knife straight through the middle of her neck.

Blood began to flow down her chest as she started to gasp for air while her body stiffened.

The Princess started to panic while she said, "Please no, please no, oh please dear heaven don't let her die."

Sadly, the princess' pleas fell on death ears as Delu's eyes slowly closed and the last sparks of life left her body. Accepting that Delu was truly gone, Akinyi felt as if her very heart had turned to stone and had begun to sink into her body as if it was drifting beneath the icy depths of the ocean.

Agyapong said, "I don't know what you're upset about. That little bitch was annoying as shit."

He walked over to Akinyi and in an authoritative tone, said, "Alright, princess, enough clowning around. Drop the dead bitch then head back to your room. We need to ask you some questions. If you're good and tell us what we want to know, then we won't tell King Ofori that your stupid ass decided to leave your room."

What was the point of me surrendering myself to the king? She carefully laid Delu's body onto the ground.

Agyapong said, "You don't need to be careful with it. We are just going to give the meat to the dogs."

Animal food. Is that all they see her as? The princess did not know why, but at that moment her tears stopped running, and a strange hollowness had taken over her.

Without a second thought, Akinyi quickly removed the knife from Delu's neck. As Delu's blood spewed out onto the floor, Agyapong shouted for Akinyi to drop the knife immediately. She ignored him, and before he could react, the princess jumped up and slashed both of his eyes.

Gyasi quickly reached for his knife, but the weapon barely made it out of its sheath when Akinyi ran her blade through his neck slicing it so deep that it was nearly disconnected from his body. Just as quickly, she pulled the blade out, and blood spewed from Gyasi's neck, forming a pool of blood, and he fell to the ground gasping for air.

Akinyi stared at Gyasi until the gasping stopped and what was left of his life was gone. Once he was dead, her attention returned to Agyapong who was on his knees screaming. She aimed her knife towards his skull, but before she could kill him, someone grabbed her arm.

The princess then heard the man she was to marry say "that's enough of that."

He took the knife from her before letting go of her arm. The moment her arm was free, Akinyi turned around looked at him. *Dammit! He's most likely very pissed, but I don't give a damn.* King Ofori walked past Akinyi before stopping and looking down at Delu's body. He continued to stare at Delu's corpse for a few minutes before turning his gaze towards Gyasi's remains. Finally, he looked at Agyapong who was still on the floor screaming.

The King smiled for reasons unknown to Akinyi which for some odd reason made her feel a little relieved. Without looking at the princess King Ofori said, "No wonder this happened." He then walked over to Agyapong and grabbed him by the neck with one hand. With practically no effort, he lifted him off the ground. Agyapong frantically thrashed around in a feeble attempt to survive.

King Ofori said, "My dear, I really must thank you for eliminating such weak men from my ranks."

Akinyi looked the king in the eyes and said, "Give me back that knife I'm not finished yet."

The king laughed again saying, "I will take over now."

He then started to slowly squeeze Agyapong neck. Agyapong started to move more frantically as he gasped for air. There was a sudden crack, followed by King Ofori dropping Agyapongs lifeless body on the ground.

Still not looking in Akinyi's direction, King Ofori said, "I will forgive you for leaving your room this time because two of my now former men broke our agreement. However, if I catch you outside your room before our wedding day again, then several citizens of what was once Enwayo will be randomly killed."

99

"What about my friend? She deserves a proper burial."

In response, King Ofori laughed as he said, "Stop being silly. My dogs should not be denied good meat."

Akinyi felt her heart sink even deeper as she accepted that there was no helping the situation.

He said, "this is why I want you to become the mother of my sons. What great warriors you and I produce. Our descendants will rule the world. You princess are a woman to be feared by the weak. Makes me excited for our wedding night even more. I suggest you hurry back to your room. Before my excitement makes me forget about tradition and rape you."

As she turned forcing herself to head back to her room, King Ofori continued to laugh. *Fucking piece of shit. I cannot wait for the day when I get to rip your throat out. Bet you won't be laughing anymore.*

The princess could still hear his laughter as she walked over to her table and fell into a chair. Tumelo stared at the princess' a sad and empty expression on his face, and at that moment, Akinyi believed that he fully understood what had happened. She could tell he felt as if he should come up with something or say anything to ease her pain; but was unable to, so they sat staring at one another as time slowly moved forward.

Chapter 17

The Kiss

The princess' bedroom slowly filled with the beautiful orange light from the sunrise. Sadly, its beauty did nothing to help Akinyi's shattered heart. She slumped in a chair, tired yet her body was unwilling to sleep. Tumelo had remained at her side throughout the night. They sat in silence until the light of morning filled the room and all signs of the night had disappeared.

Without warning, Akinyi asked, "What do I have to do for you to get rid of him?"

"I'm guessing you're talking about the king."

"Yes. What do I need to do so you will kill him and all who follow him?"

"Princess, I understand your anger, but please take a little time to calm yourself before making this kind of decision."

"Last night, right before my friend was murdered, you told me you would be willing to kill the tyrant and his followers. Why are you now so quick to change your mind?"

"I have not changed my mind about my offer. As I told you last night, I can take a life, but I do not take the action of doing so lightly. Also, you must remember that the price for me doing this for you is you agreeing to marry me."

"I know that, and I don't care. That man swore to me that he would not allow any harm to come to the people of Enwayo. Now my friend is dead all because I stupidly thought his men were too scared of him to violate his orders."

"Princess, what happened is not your fault."

I was the one who decided to blackmail those two men. It was my poor judgment that led to Delu's death. I'm not making that mistake again. "Just tell me what I have to do."

"Alright, but I can't make a deal with you at this moment." In a pissed off tone, Akinyi replied, "Why the fuck not?"

"Calm down. Just because we can't make the deal right now does not mean we can't make it later."

"You did not answer my question why can't we just make the deal now?"

"This is going to sound very silly, but it's because it's after midnight."

"That makes no sense. Why would midnight be so significant to us making a deal?"

"People call midnight the witching hour, but it's a terrible time for any magical person or creature to cast spells."

"Why?"

"Midnight causes all magic to become extremely weak. This happens because the second midnight hits it places the world in a state of being both the new day and the previous day. All magic is reliant on absolute certainty otherwise a spell cannot be cast."

"Do you mean someone casting a spell cannot have any doubt about what they are doing to use magic?"

"Yes, this is why midnight creates an interesting problem. That moment in time creates uncertainty just by being both day and night. Once midnight is passed, remnants of the distortion last until 1 a.m. Ironically, despite midnight being a time where magic is at its weakest, it is also the best time to break a curse. This is because even though all magic is weak at midnight, cursed magic is weaker than every other type of magic."

"Why does that happen?"

"No one knows and all research into that matter has been inconclusive. Anyway, even though we have to wait till midnight, breaking the curse will suck a lot of energy out of you, so I suggest you get some sleep."

"Magic sounds overly complicated."

"It is easier than it sounds, and while you're sleeping, I'm going to go out and get you a present to solidify our friendship."

"What kind of gift could you possibly give me?"

"Come on, princess. It would not be a surprise if I told you now would it."

I don't think I like the idea of him bringing me any surprises.

Tumelo hopped off of the table, and then he hopped over to the partially open balcony door. Once he was gone, the princess started to pull off her bloody nightgown. She quickly changed her mind when she realized her hands along with part of her chest and legs were covered in blood.

Akinyi forced herself to stand up then walked over to the string that was connected to a bell to ring for a servant so that they could fix her tub water. As she waited, she stared at the blood on her hands, wondering how much of it belonged to Delu and how much blood belonged to her killer. She started to feel as if she was going to start crying all over again until the door opened, taking her out of her trance.

A woman who Akinyi did not recognize walked in holding a wooden tray with a white bowl on top of it. The woman had an oval head that housed a lot of black hair which was stilted in long curls. Her eyes were a dull shade of brown. Her ears were large. She was wearing a yellow dress similar to Delu's and Serwa's. She wore a raggedy pair of leather sandals.

103

The woman looked at the princess for a moment before handing her the tray while she said, "Here, eat it."

Akinyi looked back at the woman confused, then noticed that the woman was immediately heading out of the room.

Quickly, Akinyi said, "Where do you think you are going?"

The woman turned around, put her hands on her hips, and in a very rude voice, said, "What the fuck else do you want? I already brought your breakfast."

In a pissed off tone, Akinyi responded, "Well, I don't know, bitch. How about you tell me who the fuck you are, and what you're doing here first. And for future reference, never enter my room without knocking first."

"The name is Honey, and the king assigned me to be your new personal maid."

Must be the so-called maid Delu was complaining about. Why did the usurper decide he needed her to be my maid?

Akinyi said, "Alright, you clearly don't want this job, so why don't we have someone else do it?"

The woman rolled her eyes then said, "As much as I would like that I can't. The king was very insistent that I take this job and only a dumbass would tell him no."

"Alright, I want you to get warm water for my tub."

"Didn't you take a bath yesterday?"

"Well, I thought since I'm covered in blood it would be a good idea to take another one. Also, how do you know when I do or do not bathe?"

"His majesty is very particular about his things. So, he was happy to know you liked to bath often. When this job was forced on me, I was told that I would not have to have your tub filled today."

"Well I guess it stinks to be you right now."

"Whatever! You spoiled little bitch I'll go get your stupid bathwater. As to anything else you may need, you're a big girl handle it yourself."

Akinyi sat the bowl on the table, grabbed the tray, and ran over to Honey. She tackled her to the ground and began beating her on the head.

As she did so, she screamed at Honey, "I am a Princess, and I will not be spoken to disrespectfully by a nothing like you. You will do as you are told or get the hell out of my palace."

Honey screamed as she struggled to free herself. Finally, Akinyi whacked Honey one time hard on the butt and freed her. Honey crawled towards the door righting herself as he went. When she got to the door, she turned a frightened look on her face and said, "You're crazy."

Akinyi threw the tray as Honey hurriedly ran out of the room closing the door behind her. The princess sat on the floor and laughed and cried at the same time. She felt her muscles tense up as she rose off the floor and dragged her body over to the couch before sitting down.

Call me a bitch will she well I'll teach her just how much of a bitch I can be. Worry about her later. The only thing I need to worry about now is this deal with Tumelo. I wonder if I should just wait for Bonsu to send aid. Still doing that means having to wait and I don't know if I can bear to do that anymore.

As she meditated on the matter, her stomach started to growl. In response, she walked over to the table. As the princess sat in a chair, she stared at the white substance in the bowl, wondering what it was. This looks nothing like the food the cook makes. *Shit. This does not look as good as the stuff I can cook myself.* She told herself just eat it until she realized Honey had not given her a spoon. Having no desire to deal with her again, Akinyi decided drink her breakfast. The princess held the bowl up to her lips.

The second the substance touched her tong she immediately cringed so bad she had to put the bowl down quickly otherwise she would drop it. Starting to feel like she was going to be sick from the taste, she rushed over to her camber pot and spat it out. Akinyi then retrieved a handkerchief that was sitting on her nightstand. *That was super gross. She might think that she is accomplishing something by giving me bad food. She's going to be sorry she did it.* The princess reclaimed her seat on the couch, trying to ponder the situation and her decision. However, tiredness quickly settled in, causing her to fall into a deep sleep.

Akinyi opened her eyes and noticed the beautiful light of twilight painting her bedroom walls. Slowly, she stood up then looked at her bloody hands. Her body instantly started to shake while tears rolled down her face. *Did I fall asleep with Delu's blood on me? What the hell is wrong with me? She was my friend.*

Just then she heard Owusu ask, "Akinyi, are you alright?"

Before she could try to respond, he quickly hugged her tightly in his arms, which made Akinyi's shaking come to a halt. More tears fell from her eyes as she held onto him even tighter as if he was the only person who could keep her from falling. A few minutes passed, and the princess finally calmed herself down.

She looked at Owusu with very sad eyes and said, "Delu, she, she, she…"

"I know what happened."

"How did you know one of King Ofori's men killed Delu?"

"This morning, the usurper had his men gather in the main hall where he spoke about what happened. He did not mention Delu by name, but he did say enough for me to put two and two together and that he had to kill the man who did it."

"Why did he lie about ending the life of Delu's killer?"

"He was lying?"

"I killed Gyasi for killing Delu. Then I tried to kill Agyapong, but the usurper stopped me and killed Agyapong himself."

"Despite his lie, King Ofori also threatened to burn alive anyone who disobeyed his orders not to attack any Enwayo civilians. As to whatever else he told them I did not stay to hear."

"Why?"

"I wanted to save Delu's body from becoming dog food. Thankfully I was not too late to recover her remains."

"Where is her body now?"

"I took her body to her family, so they can lay her to rest."

"Thank you."

"No problem. She was my friend too. I don't even know how I'm going to write her husband about this."

"Don't worry about writing General Idris just yet. If he finds out she is gone now, he will be too heartbroken to think clearly in battle."

In a sad voice, Owusu exclaimed, "I agree, but I just can't shake the feeling I could have done something to prevent this."

Akinyi thought, *You couldn't, but I could have. The deal is the only good option.* She looked at Owusu with very sad eyes before drawing him into a deep kiss. As she felt the softness of his lips and the warmth of his body, she could feel her heart shatter all over again. *This is truly our last kiss. Dammit! Why does life have to be so cruel?*

When they separated, Akinyi refused to look at Owusu as she said, "Someone is probably going to come to check on me soon."

"I know, but I will be back first thing tomorrow."

Akinyi wanted to remain in Owusu's strong embrace. So, when he finally let go of her she felt as if she was going to fall to the ground. But she forced herself to stand firm as she bid Owusu goodbye. One minute after he disappeared through the secret passage. For the first time since Enwayo had been captured, she felt truly alone.

At first, she thought she would cry again but whatever tears she had finally ran out leaving her with pure rage. After a few minutes of frustrated pacing, she decided to relax she would call the servants, so she could take a much-needed bath. Even if it meant she would have to deal with that bitch Honey again.

Luckily for Akinyi, Serwa came instead of Honey. Akinyi thought, *Thank goodness I hope that I have seen the last of that bitch.* She noticed that Serwa's eyes were bloodshot from crying. Akinyi knew that those tears had been for Delu.

When Serwa arrived, she came with a large tray stacked with two plates containing ribeye steaks with a side of roasted potatoes and two large bowls of salad. As soon as Akinyi saw the food, she realized she was starving.

Akinyi asked, "How are you holding up?"

"Don't worry about me. As sad as I am about Delu's murder, I know I need to be doing what little I can to help rid our land of those invaders. It's the only real way to honor her memory."

"Ok, but don't do anything too risky."

"Don't worry princess. After my brothers fell in battle fighting the usurper's army, I'm all my parents have left." Serwa started to light the bedroom candles as she continued to say, "So I will not be doing anything dangerous. Speaking of risky, when you called for assistance, I heard you had to deal with Honey this morning."

"Who told you about that?"

"My father. This morning the staff was stretched thin. Honey was the only one available to bring you breakfast. She supposedly refused to bring you the nice breakfast that my father made for you."

"That explains that nasty mess she expected me to eat earlier."

"Sorry about that no one should have to eat raw overly peppered grits."

"That stuff was grits?"

"Yep, my father wanted to bring you the better breakfast he made, but you know the usurper won't allow men anywhere near your room. Then when someone was available to bring you real food, you were asleep. It was decided to wait until you woke up to bring you something to eat. Also, everyone knew you would want to take a bath, and a few maids should be here soon with fresh water for your tub."

"Thank you, but why did no one tell the king that Honey was trying to starve me."

Serwa lit the last candle while saying, "My father considered it, knowing how important you are to the King, but the King seems extremely angry."

"So?"

"Your deal with him may still be holding strong. However, according to my father, the usurper was acting as if he heard one more piece of bad news, he would kill the messenger."

"We have to wait for one of his men to get axed before we tell him anything."

"While we are talking about this, do you have any idea why she was so desperate to try and get me to eat that mess?"

"I have not a clue. Father said that when she returned to the kitchen, she was screaming about how crazy you were."

Akinyi smiled, "yes, I taught her a lesson in simple respect. I did my best to beat it into her head. She said that she is never coming back to your room again."

"I am sure that she does not want to but she will."

"I understand that everyone believes that she is a spy for the King."

"Yes, everyone does. Anyway, your highness, if you don't need anything else, I will get back to my duties."

After Serwa was gone, the princess looked at her food then she looked at her hands. *There were times after a battle when I had to eat with bloody hands. There is no way I can eat if this is Delu's blood.* She checked her pitcher to see if there was any water inside. Thankfully, there was some water left in the pitcher.

After going out onto her deck to clean her hands, she noticed two guards standing in a section of the garden near the balcony. Deciding to take out some of her frustration on the guards, she dumped the reaming water in the guard's direction. When the water hit the guards, they immediately started to curse at the princess while other guards in the garden laughed at them.

Akinyi smiled as she whispered, "Got them this time, Delu."

Then she headed inside to eat.

After Akinyi had eaten, and her bath had been drawn, she sat in her tub, making sure she washed off all of the blood. Once she was certain all of the blood was gone, unlike her usual baths, Akinyi climbed out of the tub, instead of trying to soak and relax.

After changing into a pink dress, she wondered why Tumelo had not returned, especially since he did not seem the type to miss a meal. Figuring there was no point in worrying about a magic frog, she walked out onto her balcony and looked up at the starry night sky. Akinyi started to wonder if she was making the right decision. Sure, she wanted the king gone, but she also knew that she was not sure she could trust Tumelo.

Her thought process was interrupted when she heard Tumelo say, "Are you ready for your gift princess?"

Akinyi turned around and saw Tumelo sitting on top of a giant red box.

In a surprised voice the princess said, "How in the world did you buy me something and get it wrapped. Better yet, why did I not notice you bringing it up here?"

Tumelo hopped off of the box, and once he was on the ground, he said, "Magic. Anyway, I picked you up something I know you want."

The princess reached down to take the top off the box while wondering what he got her. Akinyi pulled off the top of the box. She looked down and saw the disfigured body of General Opoku inside. The princess strangely could not hold back her smile as she stared at the general's disfigured remains. Her joy was quickly followed by an overwhelming sense of relief. If Tumelo could take out just one of King Ofori's top men this easily, then there is no questioning that he could easily get rid of the rest.

Tumelo said, "I can see it in your eyes."

"See what?"

"That all doubt about our deal has been removed from your mind."

"You're a magic frog. I never questioned whether or not you could do the job."

"Yes, but I couldn't tell that you had doubts as to whether or not you trusted me enough to make such a life-changing deal with me. As I told you earlier, when it comes to magic, you have to be completely certain for it to work."

111

"I understand that, but umm so what are we going to do with the general?"

"Once I am human again, I will bury him in the forest. Then I will ask his ancestors to guide his soul into the next life."

"I did not take you for a man of faith."

"I told you I do not take ending a life lightly. And asking for the safety of the soul of the life that I took is my way of doing penance."

The princess replaced the lid of the box while Tumelo hopped onto the banister and stared up at the night sky. The princess walked next to him and looked at the lake as it sparkled in the moonlight.

After a minute, Tumelo said, "In less than one minute, I will be human again. I've dreamed of this day for so long, and now that it's happening. I can barely contain my excitement."

"How do you know that it will be midnight in less than a minute?"

"It's a spell I cast on myself years ago, so I always know what time it is."

"That sounds pretty handy."

"It is. Anyway, it's time to break the curse."

"Alright do we need to say anything?"

"No, you already agreed to be my wife, so all we have to do now is kiss."

"Ok."

Akinyi offered Tumelo her hand, and he hopped into her palm. She told herself a quick peck would do the trick, and she leaned in to give him a kiss. The moment her lips touched the frog's mucus skin, she instantly became so dizzy that she dropped him. The world started to spin around, and for some reason, she could hear the beating of drums.

Whether or not the drums were playing music or they were sending a message, she was too dizzy to be sure. *Dammit, What have I done?* Akinyi eventually lost her balance and hit the balcony floor hard. The moment she landed on the ground, her body was enveloped in horrible pain, and she started screaming in absolute distress. This went on until someone grabbed her and lifted her off the ground. As soon as she felt their touch, the pain went away.

When the dizziness finally ended, simultaneously, her heart stopped because she was face to face with a giant naked man. The man. The man had short curly black hair on his head and a small black beard on his chin. His skin was a silky-smooth brown he had very serious dark brown eyes. The princess stared back at the man in fear as she started to notice her skin felt very oily and her feet and hands were for some reason very sticky.

Finally, the man spoke, and in a soft voice, he said, "What to do with you?"

Fear washed over the princess, and very quickly she said, "RIBBIT. RIBBIT. RIBBIT."

In response, the man smiled, and the princess felt more scared because she realized who he was. *He must be Tumelo but if he is holding me in the air then what am I?* Akinyi looked around and saw that her clothes were on the ground and all of her deck furniture was huge. She looked back at Tumelo, completely scared because she had finally accepted that she had been transformed into the frog.

To Be Continued

In

Curse of the Frog Prince

Part 2

Want to learn more about me and my books?

You can find out on my social media.

YouTube: Madam Crystal Butterfly

Instagram: mcbutterfly777

Made in the USA
Columbia, SC
08 September 2022

66807267R00079